The
Ghosts of
Petroglyph Canyon

By

Christopher Cloud

To the Pablo Perez' of the World

Chapter 1

"Pablo, don't move!" Pia Perez rose up in the saddle and pointed. "There's a really big snake by your feet!"

His sister's terrified warning caught Pablo mid-stride and he froze, one foot suspended above the sandy riverbed. The brown and white stallion Pablo was leading by the reins lifted his head, ears erect and nostrils flaring. Sensing danger, the big horse named Buster made a strange grunting noise and pawed at the sand.

"Pablo, I think it's a rattlesnake!" Pablo's cousin yelled from the back of her gray mare. Kiki's face was scrunched up in a frightful grimace.

Pablo searched the floor of the barren wash, his heart about to jump out of his chest. Inch by inch, and ever so slowly, Pablo lowered his foot until it rested on the dusty riverbed.

"To your right!" Kiki shouted, using her hat to shade her eyes from the blazing New Mexico sun.

Twelve-year-old Pablo heard the snake before he saw it.

He recognized the one-of-a-kind sound immediately and it made his skin crawl. He looked on the ground to his right and there it was! The big Diamondback was coiled perfectly in the shade of a prickly pear cactus not three feet away. Flicking its ghastly pitchfork tongue at Pablo, the snake's deadly rattle broke the morning hush. The pasty-white noisemaker was the size of Pablo's thumb.

Pablo stared at the snake, and the snake stared back.

Kiki's gray mare named Queen Mary shook her head skittishly. "It's okay, big girl," Kiki murmured in her distinctive raspy voice, her eyes riveted on the snake.

"Easy, Pablo," Pia said in little more than a whisper, her eyes swimming in tears. "Please, please don't get bit." Pablo's nine-year-old sister covered her mouth with her hand and choked back a sob.

"It'll be okay, Pia," Pablo said, his breath coming in short, nervous spurts.

"Don't make any quick moves," Kiki warned, her laser-like gaze fixed on the angry snake.

"I hadn't planned to," Pablo said deliberately, goose-flesh chilling his bare arms. He wondered if the snake's fangs could penetrate his leather boots. Uncle Antonio had outfitted each of them with the high-top footwear for this very reason —as protection against rattlesnake bites.

"Pablo," Kiki began, her voice growing louder with each word, "the snake looks like it's going to—"

"—to what?" Pablo said, not daring to take his eyes off the deadly rattler, which had drawn back its head as if it meant business, its split tongue continuing to taste the air.

"TO STRIKE!" Kiki screamed.

The leather reins Pablo was holding suddenly drew taut. Buster was backing away. Pablo held firm to the reins and allowed the big stallion to slowly pull him out of harm's way.

"Good, Buster," Pablo said quietly. "Good horse."

"Keep going, Pablo," Pia pleaded in a soft voice, some of the worry leaving on her toast-brown face.

Short Stuff, the spotted Pinto pony on which Pia sat, had also heard the dangerous rattle—it was the reptile's way of saying: "I'm warning you! Don't come any closer!"—and the pintsize mare threw back her head with an anxious whinny.

"It's okay, Short Stuff," Pia said, leaning down and giving her pony a comforting pat on the neck. Short Stuff shuffled her hoofs uneasily.

Pablo, his sister and cousin had arrived at the Bar-7 ranch the previous day to help their Uncle Antonio with the annual June gathering. They had made the non-stop flight from Kansas City, and met their Uncle Antonio at the Albuquerque International Airport.

"Another couple of steps, Pablo," Kiki encouraged.

Out of school for the summer, the three young explorers had scheduled an afternoon of wilderness sightseeing before the gathering was to begin the next day. (Pablo had called it a "roundup" during the sixty-mile drive from the Albuquerque airport to the Bar-7 ranch. Uncle Antonio had corrected him immediately: "It's a gathering, Pablo, not a roundup. A round-up is a Hollywood word. Real cowboys call it a gathering.")

Now, at a safe distance from the deadly snake, Pablo exhaled an uneasy breath, and led Buster over to where Pia and Kiki sat atop their mounts. Pablo removed his cowboy hat and wiped the sweat from his forehead with the back of his hand. He looked up at his sister and cousin, an awkward smile on his lips. In a jittery voice he said, "Uncle Antonio was right. This place is crawling with rattlesnakes."

"That was close, Pablo," Kiki observed.

"You shouldn't have been walking your horse, Pablo!" his sister complained. She placed her hand over her heart. "I can feel my heart beating!"

"Buster was tired," Pablo said, noting the lather on the horse's neck. "I was letting him cool down."

"Please be more careful," Pia said in a motherly tone.

Pablo mounted Buster, and they continued west along Dry Creek, which stretched across the high-plains prairie as far as the eye could see. Pablo cast a parting glance at the Diamondback rattler. It was gone.

And don't come back! Pablo thought, laughing inwardly.

***

Uncle Antonio had instructed them to follow Dry Creek west. "It'll take you right to the mouth of Petroglyph Canyon," he had explained. "Big cottonwood near the canyon entrance. Locals call it *Arbol Grande*. That's Spanish for Big Tree."

Following the dusty riverbed, they arrived at the mouth of the canyon fifteen minutes after their frightening encounter with the rattlesnake. They peered warily into the backcountry ravine.

"It looks creepy," Pia observed softly, pushing her straw hat back on her head and peering into the dark shadows. Pia turned to her brother. "Don't you think it looks creepy, Pablo?"

Pablo sized up the canyon. "A little." Although the narrow entrance of the box canyon was completely in shadows, Pablo could make out the canyon's interior walls, which were tiered with vivid colors of silver and bronze. The bright ribbons of color shimmered under the scorching midday sun.

"Let's ride in," Pia suggested happily.

"I thought you said it looked creepy," Pablo said. He took a sip of water from his canteen. The water was warm but wet. "It's either creepy or it's not creepy. Which is it?"

"Yeah, it's creepy, but I really want to see those rock pictures. Uncle Antonio said they were seventy-thousand-years old."

"He did not," Pablo said, rolling his eyes.

"Uh-huh."

"Seven thousand years, not seventy thousand."

"Well, that's still pretty old." Pia looked to Kiki for backup. "Isn't it?"

"Yeah, it is," thirteen-year-old Kiki said. "I researched petroglyphs online before leaving home, and one website said that there aren't any rock-art sites older than seven thousand years anywhere in North America."

"How cool is that?" Pablo crowed.

Kiki looked at Pia. "But Uncle Antonio also said he'd be done hauling water to his cattle by noon and that we should wait for him at the mouth of the canyon," she reminded her cousin. "He said for us not to go in alone because it wasn't safe, remember?"

"Why isn't it safe?" Pia asked, wrinkling her nose.

Kiki shrugged. "I don't have a clue, but I think we should wait for him." She glanced at her watch: 11:45 a.m. "He should be here soon."

Pia agreed with a frown.

They started to dismount when a soft, moaning howl washed out of the canyon. Buster's ears perked up, and the big stallion immediately turned his head toward the strange sound.

"W-What was that?" Pia asked, her eyes fixed on the yawning mouth of the canyon.

"Probably a ghost," Pablo said. He strummed the air with his fingers and made a ghostly sound.

Pia Perez turned in her saddle and gave her older brother a sour look. "Stop that, Pablo!"

Pablo replied with a gentle laugh. "It was the wind, Pia. There's no such thing as ghosts."

"Are you just saying that or do you really mean it?"

"I really mean it."

"We should stay right here until Uncle Antonio arrives," Kiki said cautiously, snatching another wary glance of the shadowy canyon entrance. "Pia's right. It does look sort of creepy. Besides, I'm hungry. Let's eat."

With the noontime sun beating down on them, they dismounted and sat in the shade of *Arbol Grande,* which towered more than sixty feet. They tied their horses to one of the lower branches. Aunt Helen had packed them a lunch, and they sat under the tree and rifled through the brown paper sacks.

"How hot do you think it is, Pablo?" Kiki asked, wiping her brow and sitting Indian-style in the sand. She found a peanut butter and honey sandwich in her lunch sack and fanned herself with her hat as she ate it.

"Close to ninety-five," Pablo replied, gazing at the quivering fingers of heat rising from the dry riverbed. He was sitting with his back against *Arbol Grande*. The tree felt good at his back.

"Is that why Uncle Antonio has to haul water to his

cattle?" Pia asked. "Because it's so hot?" She had settled in at the base of the tree beside her brother.

"Sort of," Pablo replied. "He hauls water to his stock tanks because all the ponds are dry. It hasn't rained in a long time in this part of New Mexico." They had ridden past several dry Bar-7 lagoons on their way to Petroglyph Canyon. A cracked shell of brick-hard mud covered the bottom of what had once been small ponds.

Kiki lowered her voice to mimic their Uncle Antonio. "A hundred and fourteen days without rain." She laughed softly. "He must have said that a dozen times on the drive from Albuquerque."

"But it's probably nothing to laugh about," Pablo said gently.

Kiki nodded. "You're right, Pablo. There's nothing funny about a drought. Those poor cattle."

During the horseback ride to the canyon, they had seen dozens of whiteface cattle searching for a blade or two of grass to eat, but the pastures were brown and brittle. Pablo wondered how they managed to stay alive.

Out the corner of his eye—at the top of the canyon wall —Pablo saw something move. When he turned for a better look, it was gone. He got up and went over to where Buster was tied. He rummaged through his saddlebag and removed a pair of 8X binoculars. He immediately trained the powerful binoculars on the canyon rim. Whoever or whatever he'd seen had disappeared.

"What are you looking at, Pablo?" Pia asked.

"Just sightseeing," he said, placing the binoculars back in his saddlebag. Pablo returned to his place under the cotton-wood tree.

A small, harmless tornado-like wind called a dust devil churned along the dry riverbed before them. From under the shade of the big cottonwood tree, they watched the dust devil enter the canyon and disappear.

"What goes in doesn't come out," Pablo observed mys-teriously.

"That's not even funny, Pablo," Kiki said.

Pablo flashed an impish grin. "I couldn't resist."

"You are so lame," Pia noted, giving her brother a look.

Pablo merely laughed.

Kiki was digging through her lunch sack and looking for something else to eat when she turned to Pablo and said, "Do you get the strange feeling that we're being watched?"

Pablo nodded. "Yeah." He gestured at the rim of the canyon with the remains of his sandwich. "Up there."

"I'm pretty sure I saw somebody crouched behind a boulder," Kiki said, training her eyes on the lip of the high canyon wall, a hundred feet above.

"I'm not sure what it was, but I saw…something," Pablo said uncertainly.

"Well, I didn't see anything," Pia reported. She plucked an apple slice from a cellophane baggie. "Except cows and rattlesnakes, that is." She popped the apple slice into her mouth, pulled her Nintendo DS out of her shirt pocket and began playing.

Pablo shot his sister a disapproving frown. "We fly all the way to New Mexico, Pia, to ride and rope and visit the great Southwest, and you're playing Nintendo?"

"That's right, Pablo! We flew all the way to New Mexico to ride and rope and—"

"Okay! Okay!" Sometimes his sister was impossible.

Kiki spotted something unusual nearby, and she said: "Pablo, what's that?"

Pablo followed his cousin's gaze to a set of deep imprints in the sand thirty feet away.

Pablo and Kiki got up and walked over to the imprints and investigated. A dozen or so sandy impressions had been made in sets of two. Each furrow was about six inches deep, a foot wide, and ten feet long. The imprints covered an area about the size of a large classroom.

"Any ideas?" Pablo asked.

Kiki studied the deep impressions. "Not at the moment. You?"

Pablo shook his head. "Hmm. Not really."

"Did some sort of animal make them?" Kiki asked,

gently dragging the toe of her boot through one of the deep grooves.

"What'd you have in mind?" Pablo continued to study the imprints.

"You're the male in the group. You should know all about animal signs."

Pablo looked up with a small laugh. "These were not made by an animal. How's that?"

"Okay…for the moment."

They returned to the shade of the cottonwood tree.

"Pablo," Pia said, stowing her Nintendo and motioning toward the rim of the canyon, "if someone is up there, why would they be watching us?"

"Don't know."

"I wish Uncle Antonio would get here," Pia said, an anxious glint in her eyes.

"He'll be here any minute," Pablo said, looking down Dry Creek.

"Are you just saying that or do you really—"

"I really mean it."

Chapter 2

"Watch your step!" Uncle Antonio called back to them with a wave of his cane. "Not far now!"

Pablo, Pia, and Kiki followed close on their uncle's heels.

Huge slabs of sandstone had pulled away from the Petroglyph Canyon walls over thousands of years, and the jagged ruins extended halfway to the top of the high walls. Large piñon trees had somehow managed to take root in the steep, craggy debris field.

Uncle Antonio had arrived five minutes earlier after driving his water truck down Dry Creek and parking it near the canyon entrance not far from the huge cottonwood. A tall, lanky man, Uncle Antonio was never without his soiled, gray cowboy hat. No one could ever remember seeing Uncle Antonio without his hat, and one of his ranch hands had claimed years earlier that the owner of the Bar-7 actually slept in it.

Many of the boulders in Petroglyph Canyon—both large

and small—were broken and cracked, most with sharp edges, and each step required their full attention. The rocky, uneven terrain was not suitable for horses, and they had left their mounts tied in the shade of *Arbol Grande*.

"Not far now," Uncle Antonio said.

"I'll bet they're going to be beautiful!" Pia gushed.

"They're all of that, Pia," Uncle Antonio said, glancing back at his niece. "You won't be disappointed."

Uncle Antonio walked with a cane these days. He had been kicked in his knee the year before by an angry bull calf during the annual gathering, and the knee had not healed well.

"Are they distinct?" Kiki asked. "I'd like to get some photos."

"Oh, they're distinct, alright," Uncle Antonio replied.

"What's distinct?" Pia asked.

"Really clear," Kiki said. "Easy to see."

"Oh."

With his nephew and nieces in tow, Uncle Antonio stepped around the corpse of a Pronghorn antelope.

"Poor devil," Uncle Antonio observed sadly, waving his cane over the carcass. "Hard to figure."

"Why?" Pablo asked, gazing at the tan and white remains. Flies had found the dead animal and were making a feast of it.

"Antelopes don't frequent this canyon." Uncle Antonio

pointed at the canyon rim with his cane. "They stay up top on the prairie."

"How'd it get down here?" Pia said, surveying the dead animal and making the kind of unpleasant face only a nine-year-old could make.

"That's my point," Uncle Antonio said. "Pronghorns are as sure-footed as mountain goats. Doesn't make any sense. This is the third antelope I've found dead in the canyon in the past month. Someone is driving them over the cliff's edge." Uncle Antonio looked up at the canyon rim.

"That's sad," Pia said, her eyes fixed on the antelope's remains.

"Yes, it is, Pia," Uncle Antonio agreed. "Who would want to hurt an innocent animal?"

Uncle Antonio removed his soiled cowboy hat and shook his head gloomily. "Something up top must have really spooked her. No way she fell to her death accidentally."

Stepping around the carcass, they hiked on.

"Newspaper Rock! Not far now!" Uncle Antonio said. "I think you'll be surprised!"

Pia squealed when a lizard slithered into a rocky crack inches from her feet.

Uncle Antonio laughed over his shoulder. "Nothing to fear, Pia. Just a plain old collared lizard. The slithery devils are everywhere. They're harmless. It's the rattlesnakes we need to watch out for."

They continued to climb the mountain of rubble.

"Watch your head!" Uncle Antonio warned seconds later, disappearing into a shadowy passageway that had been formed by a collection of several large boulders. Brought together by the relentless force of gravity, the huge boulders had merged to form the dusky cavern.

They ducked inside behind their uncle. The cave offered some relief from the noontime heat. Pablo guessed it was fully twenty degrees cooler inside the small cavern.

"Getting close!" Uncle Antonio crowed.

Emerging on the opposite side of the rocky chamber, Uncle Antonio crawled up a craggy staircase of boulders. Using his cane for leverage, he paused every few steps to allow his bad knee to rest. Pablo, Pia, and Kiki scurried up the rocks behind him.

When Uncle Antonio reached the top of the rocky stairs, he balanced himself on an uneven ledge with his cane, his eyes fixed on an immense, inward-facing boulder a few yards away.

"Newspaper Rock," Uncle Antonio announced proudly. His spectacles had slipped down his nose and he took a moment to push them up. "All the latest news of the day… several thousand years ago, that is."

Crowding in beside their uncle on the stone balcony, they saw what he saw. Before them were dozens of mysteri-

ous petroglyphs, which had been etched into the even face of
the huge sandstone panel.

The hair on the back of Pablo's neck stiffened, and the
whites of Pia's eyes doubled in size. A soft and raspy "Awesome!" slipped from Kiki's lips, and she immediately raised
her camera and began taking pictures. The light was perfect.

Pablo couldn't take his eyes off the rock drawings before
him. They were spectacular. The peculiar sandstone sketches
were all that Uncle Antonio had promised. Many of the
beautiful designs were true works of art. Pablo tried to soak it
all in—his eyes darted from one etching to another.

Newspaper Rock was huge, twenty feet by twenty feet,
Pablo calculated, and covered from top to bottom with eerie,
primitive drawings. Pablo counted forty-eight. The prehistoric
art was more than spectacular. It was super-spectacular. He
had never seen anything like it in his life.

"Surprised?" Uncle Antonio asked, his eyes showing the
delight he felt.

"Very," Pablo replied.

"Me, too," Pia said.

"Awesome," Kiki repeated.

A few of the wonderful stone pictures were easy for
Pablo to identify: a stalk of corn; a large flying bird; a herd of
elk; a small handprint; a four-legged creature resembling an
anteater; a human figure, arms raised above its head as if in
celebration.

Other drawings were baffling: a row of seven triangles, each about the size of a soccer ball except for the last, which was about the size of a softball; three six-foot-long wavy lines; a circle with a dot in its center; circles within circles; a peculiar hourglass-like figure. They were all very odd, Pablo thought, and as he inspected the peculiar wavy lines, the strange circles within circles, he couldn't help but wonder: *What were the makers of these strange pictures trying to say?*

"Archaic Style," Uncle Antonio said, leaning across the narrow void that separated them from the marvelous petroglyphs. He touched the set of strange wavy lines with the tip of his cane. "Archaic Style means they are very, very old."

Kiki took notes on her phone. She planned to write a story for her school newspaper when classes resumed in the fall. Pablo shot a few pictures with his phone.

"Ar-what, Uncle?" Pia asked.

"Archaic," Uncle Antonio said. "That means they were created between five thousand years B.C. and three hundred years A.D." He swept the air with his cane. "Some of these glyphs could be as old as seven thousand years. That's around the time of the Stone Age."

"Wow!" Pia chimed.

As Pablo continued to admire the strange glyphs, he was distracted again by something moving on the rim above. This time he saw the figure clearly—it was a man! A man wearing an eye patch! *An eye patch*? Pablo thought. *Too weird*! Pablo was certain the heat was playing tricks with his eyes, and he blinked several times and then looked again. Mr. Eye Patch was gone.

"How'd they make them?" Pia asked, her eyes fixed on the huge sandstone panel.

"One rock as a hammer, another sharper rock as a chisel," Uncle Antonio explained, using his hands to demonstrate. "Wasn't easy. No metal tools back in those days, Pia." He teetered forward and the tip of his cane moved up the boulder to a pair of handprints. "These are not so old. These are from the Anasazi Style. From about three hundred A.D. to thirteen hundred A.D."

Pia successfully repeated the word Anasazi, slowly mouthing each syllable.

Kiki stared at the stone pallet Uncle Antonio called Newspaper Rock. "Are you saying these drawings were done over a period of hundreds, maybe thousands of years?"

"You betcha! Thousands of years," her uncle cheered. "Maybe two dozen generations of Native Americans once lived in this beautiful canyon."

Pablo could see the satisfaction Uncle Antonio took in explaining the rock drawings. It showed in his eyes.

Kiki collected the information on her phone, her fingers busily tapping the keys.

"This is one of my favorites," Uncle Antonio said, gesturing toward a horned and muscular humanlike figure.

The ghostly illustration was the largest picture on the rock and measured nearly four feet tall. "I call it Charles Atlas With Horns."

"Charles Atlas?" Pia said. "Who's that?"

"He was muscleman from maybe fifty years ago," Pablo said. "He used to be skinny and other men would kick sand in his face at the beach, but then he started working out and developed huge muscles. After that, nobody kicked sand in his face."

Pia looked at her brother with a blank expression. "That's a really stupid story, Pablo."

Pablo grinned. "Yeah, I suppose it is."

"Was Charles Atlas real?" Pia asked.

Pablo shrugged. "I'm not sure."

Uncle Antonio smiled. "I don't know if Charles Atlas was real, Pia, but this petroglyph is sure enough real. To me, Charles Atlas With Horns is a majestic work of art, and no less a masterpiece than a Renoir."

Kiki saw the bewildered expression on Pia's face, and she said, "Renoir was a famous French painter. He was also real."

Pablo saw movement again on the east rim of the canyon. Yes! The man was wearing an eye patch! Then the man was gone. Pablo immediately looked at Kiki.

Kiki nodded with a puzzled look on her face. "I saw him too, Pablo."

"Saw what?" Uncle Antonio said, turning toward them.

"Someone at the top of the canyon," Pablo said, motioning.

"The heat does funny things in this canyon," Uncle Antonio said casually, gazing at the top of the canyon rim. "Creates mirages."

"I don't think it was a mirage," Kiki said.

"Maybe a Pronghorn," their uncle said, shading his eyes from the sun and having a look himself.

Pablo nodded. "Maybe." *Yeah, a Pronghorn with an eye patch.*

Pablo turned his attention back to the sandstone illustrations. "What were they trying to say, Uncle Antonio?"

"I've asked myself the same question, Pablo," he replied. "But I don't think they were trying to say anything. They were saying it. We just can't decode it." Uncle Antonio removed his soiled gray hat again, plucked a white hankie out of his shirt pocket, and wiped the sweat from his forehead. "They were telling the stories of their lives: We planted corn. My wife bore a son. The earth trembled. Our chief died. I killed a deer. A bright light fell from the sky." Antonio Flores turned back toward Newspaper Rock. "Like I said, they're telling stories, we just can't read them. For every glyph, so they say," he said, "there is its maker, and this maker still lives within the walls of this canyon."

"I don't understand," Pia said.

"The spirits of the glyph makers dwell in the canyon," Uncle Antonio said.

Pia's eyes got round. "Do you mean like…like ghosts?"

"It's just a story, Pia," her uncle said. "I wouldn't be too concerned."

"I won't," she said softly.

"Newspaper Rock is the good news," Uncle Antonio said, heaving a big sigh. "Now for the bad news."

Chapter 3

They descended the mountain of sandstone rubble, and were soon standing on the canyon floor.

Uncle Antonio led them to one a large boulder, which was about the size of an S.U.V. The huge boulder was covered from top to bottom and on all sides with dozens of rock drawings. Small craters about the size of dinner plates had also been carved into the Mother Rock's rust-colored skin.

"Not very pretty, is it?" Uncle Antonio said, tapping one such crater with the tip of his cane.

"No," Pablo and Kiki said together.

"Not even," Pia said.

The surgical incisions had been made at 45-degree angles, and formed a perfect hexagon.

"Looters," Uncle Antonio said, his tone strangely sad.

Pablo ran his hand over the crater. "You mean someone came in here and—"

"—and cut out a glyph," Uncle Antonio replied, moving

the tip of his cane to another crater. "This used to be a beautiful rock drawing of a buffalo with two spears in its side. The glyph was about this size." He cupped his hands together. "It was an exquisite piece of art, and one of my favorites. I'd even given it a name—Barbed Buffalo."

Pablo tried to picture the glyph in his mind.

Uncle Antonio kicked at the dirt. "It's this way for the next hundred yards or so. They started at the mouth of the canyon and are working their way to the end. Dozens of beautiful glyphs carved out."

"How do they carve them out?" Pablo said.

"That's the sixty-four thousand dollar question," Uncle Antonio said. "My best guess would be a rock saw."

"That is so not right," Kiki said, looking at the place where the Barbed Buffalo once resided. "But why are they stealing them?" She raised her camera and snapped a photo of the ugly crater.

"Money," Kiki's uncle said. "A foot-square glyph brings good money these days. Several thousand dollars, folks that know tell me." Uncle Antonio heaved a big sigh. "Damned looters." And then, looking at each of them, he said, "Excuse my language, kids."

"Maybe the police can catch them," Pia said.

Uncle Antonio shook his head. "No police in this neck of the woods, Pia. We're thirty-two miles from the sheriff's office in Sierra Vista. More than fifty miles from Santa Fe."

"Oh."

"Had the Sierra Vista county sheriff out here a time or two, but she doesn't have the manpower for any type of surveillance."

"She?" Kiki said, surprised.

"That's right. Name's Maggie Frost." Uncle Antonio uttered a healthy laugh. "Don't be fooled because she's a she. Maggie's tough as nails."

"I wonder why they haven't stolen any of the Newspaper Rock glyphs?" Pablo asked.

Uncle Antonio heaved another big sigh. "Newspaper Rock is a little tougher to get to, but they will. It's just a matter of time. They're cutting out the easy ones for now," Uncle Antonio said. "I suppose I should have all these wonderful glyphs documented. Pictures taken and such, but I simply don't have the time. You document a glyph, and the odds it will be stolen are reduced to just about zero."

"What's documenting mean?" Pia asked.

Good question, Pia, Pablo thought. He was about to ask the same thing.

"Documenting a glyph is sort of like registering it, Pia," Uncle Antonio said. "And if it's registered, no one would buy it for fear of being caught with stolen property, and if no one would buy it, no one would steal it."

"Oh."

"That makes sense," Kiki said.

"Properly documenting a glyph requires a photo, a sketch, and a GPS reading of each rock drawing. It's quite a job," Uncle Antonio continued. "If it was in my power I'd document every glyph in this canyon, but running this ranch is a fulltime job," he said. "Just me and Charlie these days. I'm hauling water and Charlie's riding fence."

"Who's Charlie?" Kiki asked. She moved in for a closer shot of the unsightly crater.

"Charlie is a cowboy that works here at the Bar-7. Good man. Hard worker." Uncle Antonio paused to clean his glasses on his shirtsleeve. "I have my suspicions about who's stealing my glyphs. No way to prove it, and besides, I'm not so sure they're smart enough." He put on his glasses, and said, "It's a bunch that lives in Axe Handle."

"That's a funny name for a town," Pia said.

"I suppose it is, Pia," her uncle said. "The town, or what's left of it, sits at the base of Burro Mountains. Used to mine silver in those mountains, and Axe Handle was a thriving little community. Not much to Axe Handle these days. A few deserted buildings. The Ragland brothers actually live in one of those deserted building." He wiped his brow again. "Clan of no-accounts. Red, Pirate, and Gordo. They'll kill a dozen or so of my cows every year about this time. Kill them and butcher them for the meat. Axe Handle isn't on my property. It's owned by the state. If it was, I'd evict those Ragland brothers *muy pronto.*"

"What kind of name is Gordo?" Pia asked.

Uncle Antonio gave a kindly smile. "That's Spanish for fat."

"What about Pirate?" Kiki asked.

"The middle brother only has one eye," Uncle Antonio said. "Wears a patch." He put his hand over one eye. "Red shot him with a bow and arrow when they were kids growing up in Albuquerque. Took an eye. Pirate looks like some sort of Hollywood buccaneer with that eye patch."

Kiki and Pablo shared a sobering glance.

"Red's the oldest. His hair is the color of spaghetti sauce," Uncle Antonio said. "He's got a temper to match. That's why I didn't want you kids coming into this canyon alone. If the Ragland brothers are the ones stealing my glyphs, I don't want you to walk up on them by surprise. No telling what they might do." Antonio Flores paused long enough to mop his brow again. "Their real names are Henry, that would be Red, Chester, that's Gordo, and Albert, that's Pirate's given name. If you ever run into them, call them by their nicknames. They don't much care for their real names."

Pablo wondered if it had been one of the Ragland brothers that they'd seen spying down on them earlier. *Silly question,* he said to himself. *How many people wear eye patches?*

"Pablo," Uncle Antonio said, his tone frightfully serious, "you kids see that Ragland bunch, you stay clear."

Pablo said that they would.

They hiked a short distance down the dusty canyon to where a second petroglyph had been cut from a smaller boulder. Several other rock drawings had been successfully removed, and all that remained were hexagon-shaped craters. The partial remains of one glyph were lying on the ground, the result of an excavation job gone wrong.

"This is all new," Uncle Antonio said, glancing at the senseless vandalism. "Must have been done in the past few days. Made a mess of this one." The partial rock drawing lay in the sand at the base of the boulder. He touched the broken piece with the end of his cane. The rock art was that of a handprint, and all that remained was half a hand and the ring and little fingers. "They must have missed it in their hurry to flee the scene of the crime."

Pia leaned down and picked up what remained of the glyph. "Can I keep it, Uncle Antonio?"

"Sure thing, Pia," her uncle replied. "It's yours to keep."

"I'm going to name it Mr. Two Fingers because he only has two fingers," Pia said with a bright smile.

"How about Mrs. Two Fingers?" Kiki suggested. "For all we know, it could have been a woman's hand etched into the rock."

Pia grinned. "Okay, Mrs. Two Fingers." She dropped the partial petroglyph into her shirt pocket.

"Good name, Pia," Uncle Antonio said. And then,

turning back to the tarnished boulder he said, "I don't know how the looters learned about this beautiful place, but I sure wish they'd go away and stay away."

"Can't you sort of…you know, stake out the canyon?" Pablo asked.

"Find a hiding place behind one of these boulders," Kiki suggested.

A gloomy smile stretched Uncle Antonio's leathery face. "Not enough hours in the day, kids. Hauling water is a fulltime job. When we leave this canyon, I'll drive back to the ranch, fill old Jezebel up with another thousand gallons of water and head out again. Still have six more tanks to fill. By the end of the day I'm plum tuckered out. My knee…"

"We could help you haul water," Pablo said eagerly.

Uncle Antonio smiled. "I appreciate the thought, Pablo, but it's a one-man job. I'll do fine."

Pablo tried to think of something to say—something that might put a positive light on a gloomy situation—but nothing came to mind. It did, however, occur to him that bringing the looters to justice might be a simple task. A person with some time on their hands, someone who had two good knees and was not tuckered out from hauling water all day, could simply stake out a spot somewhere in the canyon, and then wait and watch. It would be easy enough to get close with his camera phone for a picture. The sound of the rock saw or whatever they used to carve out the petroglyphs was probably so loud they would never hear a person sneaking close. Shoot a picture, and then call the sheriff.

Pablo's plan made perfect sense.

The tip of Uncle Antonio's cane gently brushed one of the few remaining glyphs on the boulder before them. The art represented some sort of four-legged animal with pointed ears and a long tail.

"Think about this, kids," Uncle Antonio said. "These magnificent drawings are so old that they were etched centuries before the first blocks were laid at the Giza Pyramids, maybe even before the first stone was raised at Stonehenge." He cast a mournful eye at the surrounding vandalism. "To my thinking, such ancestry deserves the kindly status reserved for popes and kings." He paused, his jaw clenched. "And that's all I'm going say on the subject. It gets me too upset."

Uncle Antonio kicked at the dusty canyon floor in disgust, and in a soft voice said, "A hundred and fifteen days without rain."

***

Pablo detailed his plan to photograph the looters to Pia and Kiki on the ride back to the Bar-7 ranch. It was met with skepticism from Kiki, support from Pia.

"That could be very dangerous, Pablo," Kiki said. "These people, these petroglyph looters, could be hardened criminals. If it is those Ragland brothers, like Uncle Antonio said, it could be hazardous to our health. And I can almost guarantee that it was the Ragland brother called Pirate that we saw today."

"Ditto that," Pablo said. "Not too many people with eye patches."

"So you actually saw him?" Pia asked.

Pablo nodded. "We actually saw him."

"I'll bet they have the canyon under surveillance," Kiki said. "I vote No on your plan. Too dangerous. I'd like to spend a worry-free vacation here at the ranch."

"I'm on Pablo's side," Pia said. "It's not fair that somebody is stealing Uncle Antonio's petro…." Pia looked at her older brother, her nose wrinkled. "What are they called, Pablo?"

"Petroglyphs."

"Yeah, petroglyphs," Pia said. "Let's hide, and when we see them, we'll take their picture and then call the sheriff." She looked at her brother. "I think it's a great plan, Pablo."

They continued on horseback down Dry Creek, the afternoon sun hot against their backs.

"Pablo, I figured out what made those depressions in the sand," Kiki said after awhile.

"What?" Pablo said.

"Skids."

"Skids?" He looked at his cousin, perplexed. "What kind of skids?"

"Helicopter."

Chapter 4

Pablo, Pia, and Kiki spent the next morning on horse-back gathering (or attempting to gather) newborn calves and their mothers from Pasture 1, the smallest of the twelve Bar-7 pastures. It measured a mere two thousand acres. Uncle Antonio told them he wanted to spare them from a day of hard riding, and he had deliberately assigned them to a smaller pasture, one with few cattle.

That plan was fine with Pablo. There was more to this gathering business than met the eye. It was hot and dusty, and the cattle seemed to have minds of their own, especially the calves. If you tried to herd them to the right, they went to the left. If you wanted to drive them north, they went south. They had stumbled upon a mother and her calf an hour earlier, but the animals had somehow managed to disappear down one of the many deep ravines that crisscrossed the Bar-7's ninety-thousand acres. Pablo dug out his binoculars, but he still couldn't locate them.

"I think they got away, Pablo," Pia said from atop Short Stuff, peering into the empty ravine.

"I think you're right," Pablo agreed, scanning the dusty ravine with the binoculars one last time.

"This is way harder than I thought," Kiki admitted from the back of Queen Mary, taking a drink from her canteen.

These were lean times for Uncle Antonio and his Bar-7 ranch. His fulltime staff of cowboys that once had totaled five had been reduced to one, and a dozen or so of his neighbors had pitched in to help gather the calves, which had been born that spring. Occasionally, Pablo would observe one or two of the volunteer cowboys at a distance in an adjacent pasture.

It was a little after ten that morning when Pia spotted the herd of Pronghorn antelope.

"Look, Pablo!" Pia squealed, raising up in her saddle and pointing. "Antelope!"

Ears at attention, heads raised, the small herd stood watching as Pablo, his sister, and cousin approached slowly on horseback. Pablo counted thirteen. Two spotted Pronghorn calves nudged in close to their mothers, their eyes glued on the advancing strangers.

"Wow, that is one beautiful herd of antelope," Kiki gushed, raising her camera and capturing some pictures.

When they were within a stone's throw of the herd, the big Alpha male, the leader of the herd, turned and sprinted away. The herd quickly followed.

"Let's race them!" Pablo cried, and he dug his heels into the sides of his brown and white Paint. Buster responded immediately, breaking into a gallop.

"Yee-ha!" Kiki exclaimed loudly, coaxing Queen Mary into a trot and then into a gallop.

"Wait for me!" Pia cried, gently slapping her pony gently on the neck with the ends of the leather reins. "Go, Short Stuff! Go!"

Over the New Mexico prairie they raced, whooping and hollering, Buster, Queen Mary, and Short Stuff kicking up chunks of sod as they sped past the many mesquite bushes and yucca plants that dotted the arid grasslands. The herd of antelope swept over the prairie before them like a tsunami, and billowing clouds of dust curled into the air behind them.

After a mile or so—Pablo noted that the foals had no problem keeping up with their mothers—the antelopes ran down an embankment and into a thicket of cottonwood trees. They leaped across a dry arroyo, and then bounded up the embankment on the other side. They were quickly out of sight.

Pablo reined in his horse at the edge of the barren arroyo. Pia and Kiki arrived moments later.

"That was fun, Pablo!" Pia squealed. "Those antelope are really fast!"

"I could get addicted to this!" Kiki said in a loud voice,

and then breaking into song: "Oh, give me a home where the antelope roam and the skies are not cloudy all day…"

Pablo laughed and started to join in the singing, but what he saw off to his right brought a frightful chill to his backbone.

Three men, their shirts and chaps soaked in blood, were bent over a dead cow less than twenty yards away. One of the men was fat. The second wore a black eye patch, and the third was redheaded. They were butchering the cow.

The Ragland brothers! Pablo thought, a sick fear knotting his stomach. Uncle Antonio was right. They were a mean-looking bunch.

Kiki asked Pablo in a low voice, "Is that who I think it is?"

"Probably," Pablo replied.

"They won't hurt us, will they, Pablo?" Pia asked, nudging her pony closer to Pablo's big stallion.

"Not if I have anything to say about it," Pablo pledged.

The men's horses were tied to a nearby tree, not far from where they stood slaughtering the cow. A mule was teetered to a stump beside the partially butchered whiteface. Gory slabs of beef were tied to the back of the mule.

His lower lip bulging with a wad of chewing tobacco, Red Ragland strolled over to where Pablo, Pia, and Kiki sat on their horses. He held a long butcher knife at his side.

"Go ahead there, little lady," Red said with a smirk. "Finish your song. I was liking it just fine."

"No, thanks," Kiki said, glaring at the rumpled cowboy.

Red's smirk soured and his angry gaze swept over each of them. He spit a wad of tobacco juice. "What are ya kids doing out here any ways? Where's your parents?"

"My parents are back in Missouri," Kiki said. "If it's any of your business."

"Our mother is back in Missouri too," Pablo said.

"We don't have a father," Pia spoke up. "He died in a car crash."

"Uh-huh," Red said. "Your kids spying on us?"

"No, we're not spying, and I could ask you—" Pablo didn't like the sound of his own voice. It sounded weak and unsure. "—and I could ask you the same question," he said in a strong and more determined voice. "This is Bar-7 land. Everything between here and Axe Handle is Bar-7 range." Pablo nodded toward the butchered cow. "And that's Bar-7 stock."

There was an awful smell in the air. Pablo decided it wasn't the dead cow. It was Red Ragland.

"What makes ya so smart, kid?" Red sneered.

Pablo glimpsed the partially butchered whiteface. He could make out the brand on the rump—the number 7 with a bar through it. "That's the Bar-7 brand," Pablo said, leveling a finger at the dead cow. "Belongs to Antonio Flores."

"That a fact?" Red spit another dirty stream of tobacco juice.

"You're pretty good at spitting, Henry Ragland," Kiki said. "World-class, I'd say."

A red flush of anger rose in Henry Ragland's face. He shook a fist at Kiki. "Don't ya be calling me that. Name's Red."

"Well, Red, that's Bar-7 beef you and your brothers are making a mess of," Kiki said, a saucy tone in her voice, her face filled with mischief.

Easy, Kiki, Pablo thought.

Red Ragland turned toward his brothers and shouted. "Hear that boys? Kids here say that there whiteface belongs to Antonio Flores."

"Well, what do you know," Gordo said, his huge belly jiggling beneath his bloody 3X-size T-shirt.

"Hard to believe, ain't it?" Red told his brother.

Butcher knife in hand, Gordo walked leisurely over to where his red-haired brother stood. (It was really more of a penguin waddle than a human walk.)

"Gordo, ya see a brand on that there moo-cow?" Red jerked a thumb over his shoulder.

"Didn't see no brand," Gordo said, wiping his bloody knife on the sleeve of his T-shirt. "It's sure enough bad timing for you kids," Gordo said gloomily, looking up at them. "Coming along like this. Bad timing, for sure."

Red yelled over to Pirate, who was cutting a chunk of beef from the carcass. "Ya see a brand on that cow, Pirate?"

Pirate adjusted the patch over his eye. "Leave the kids be, Red. They ain't a-hurting nobody."

Red looked at Kiki and grinned through horrid, tobacco-stained teeth. "That's my brother. People call him Pirate 'cause he ain't got but one eye. He's the ar-tist in the family." Red smiled like a fool. "A one-eyed ar-tist. Ain't that some-thing?"

"Yeah, that's something," Kiki mocked.

Pablo had heard enough small talk, and he gestured in the direction of the butchered whiteface. "I can see the brand from here," he repeated. "Bar-7. Plain as day."

Red Ragland stepped over to where Pablo sat atop Buster. He wiped his knife on his chaps and glared up at Pablo.

A tremble of fear arose inside Pablo, but he held Red's glare.

Finally, Red snatched a glance over his shoulder. "Ya mean that burned spot on the cow's rump?"

"Yes," Pablo replied, wondering how long Red Ragland planned to play his silly little game.

"Is that what that is?" Red asked, grinning from ear to ear.

Kiki spit out the words. "I think you know what a cattle

brand looks like, Henry Ragland. Nobody could be that...
stupid."

The veins in Red's neck swelled immediately, and he
again shook a fist at Kiki. "I done told ya once, girlie, don't
be calling me Henry, and don't be calling me stupid, neither.
And how is it ya know my name?"

"Everybody knows your name, Henry," Kiki replied
calmly. "You're very famous."

Pia uttered a nervous giggle.

Red looked at Kiki and said, "That so?"

"Sure. Henry, Chester, and Albert Ragland," Kiki continued. "We've heard all about you three." She pulled her
camera out of her saddlebag. "Mind if I snap your picture?
I'm sure the sheriff in Sierra Vista—I believe her name is
Maggie Frost—would love to see you three standing beside
that butchered Bar-7 cow." Kiki waved Gordo closer. "Gordo,
if you could move in a little closer to Red for a picture..."

"I don't think so," Gordo said, sneering.

"No pictures." Red held up his hand to hide his face.

"Kiki...?" Pablo cautioned softly. "Maybe that's not
such a good idea."

Kiki smiled craftily at Red Ragland and returned the
camera to her saddlebag. "Maybe next time, Henry, uh, that
is, Red."

Red cocked his head and looked up at Pablo, and then
spit another stream of tobacco juice onto the ground.

"Ya here for the gathering?"

"That's right," Pablo said, the fear continuing to dredge up a new reserve of courage. He had never seen two uglier, meaner looking men in his life. Red and Gordo were pure scary. Pirate wasn't much better. He wouldn't win any beauty contests either.

"Heard ya kids was in town," Red said, spitting again. Some of the juice dribbled down his whiskered jaw and he swiped at it with the back of his hand. "Related to Antonio Flores, somebody said."

Pia suddenly spoke up, her comment directed at the redheaded Ragland brother. "That'll give you cancer, mister!"

Red looked at Pia for the first time, his face drawn up in puzzlement. "Huh?"

"I said, that'll give you cancer," Pia said. "My teacher back in Missouri said chewing tobacco was bad for you. As bad as smoking."

"She did, did she?" Red seemed amused.

"I saw a picture once of a man who had chewed tobacco all his life and he had half of his jaw cut—"

"Keep it to yourself, squirt," Red said, his amusement short-lived.

"I'm no squirt!" Pia howled.

"Pirate seen ya kids poking around Petroglyph Canyon yesterday," Red told Pablo. He turned toward Pirate, who was content to engage in the squabble from a distance. "Ain't that right, Pirate?"

"That's right. Them kids was in the canyon with Antonio Flores."

"What was ya up to?" Red asked, looking up at Pablo.

Kiki didn't wait for Pablo to reply, and she said, "That would fall under the heading of None of Your Business, Henry."

Red stared up at Kiki, his eyes blazing with rage. Baring his teeth in a gruesome smile, his words came out dark and slithery. "I think ya children need to turn them there horses around and trot on back to the Bar-7. That there whiteface heifer over there ain't got no brand, leastwise none that we could make out. It's fair game. Like deer and antelope and every other critter on the prairie. If that idea don't work for ya, then maybe we'll be butchering something else besides cow."

Complete silence.

"I think we've worn out our welcome, Pablo," Kiki said softly.

"Ditto that," Pablo replied. "Let's ride."

Pia opened her mouth to say something, but Pablo gave her a quick shake of his head, as if to say, "Save it, Pia."

But Pia's words were already formed in her mouth and she had no intention of holding them back. "You'll be sorry you killed my Uncle Antonio's cow!" she yelled, wagging her finger at the two brothers.

Red and Gordo laughed like two drunkards, then Red's mood turned dark again and he said, "Don't let me catch you kids spying on us again. I won't be as pleasant next time."

Pablo dug his heels into Buster and the horse hurried into a trot. Kiki and Pia were close behind.

Red's vulgar shout resounded across the prairie. "Remember what I said!"

***

Uncle Antonio was sitting on the top rung of the corral fence when they arrived back at the ranch late that afternoon. He was making notes on a small pad. As each team of cowboys herded the yearlings and their mothers into the corral from the twelve Bar-7 pastures, Uncle Antonio tallied the number of calves. His total had reached two hundred and six. The calves and their mothers milled around inside the main cattle pen. Bulls were allowed to remain in the pasture year-round, but any that had been herded back to the ranch were fenced in a separate corral.

Pablo gave Uncle Antonio a wave as they approached.

Pablo felt a little embarrassed that he and his sister and cousin had managed to gather only a single calf and its mother. They had chased them down on the return trip to the ranch. Most of the other cowboy teams had gathered dozens of mother-calf pairs. After herding them into the corral and tying up their horses, they went over to where their Uncle Antonio sat on the corral fence.

"Well, kids, how was your first day of riding the range?" their uncle asked. He removed his hat and wiped his brow.

"We only gathered one calf and its mother, Uncle Antonio," Pia said unhappily. "The others kept running away."

Antonio laughed. "Those yearlings have a bad habit of doing that."

Pablo told his uncle about their encounter with the Ragland brothers. Uncle Antonio shook his head and said he was glad nobody was hurt.

"Like I said before. They're a mean bunch," Uncle Antonio said. "Next time you see them, just keep on riding. If the situation turns ugly, give your Aunt Helen or me a call. There's a cell tower about ten miles north of Petroglyph Canyon next to the Interstate highway. Don't give those Ragland brothers the luxury of conversation."

***

At a little before sunset, as the last team of cowboys herded their catch of calves and mothers into the huge Bar-7 corral, a lone horseman appeared on the horizon.

They watched the rider approach, shading their eyes from the setting sun.

"Charlie Pecos," Uncle Antonio said. "He rides fence for the Bar-7."

"Rides fence?" Pia asked, her forehead pleated with curiosity.

"That means he mends fences, Pia," Uncle Antonio said. "Charlie Pecos is Indian. That is, Native American. Mescalero Apache."

"I've heard of Apaches," Pia said. "But I thought that was just in the movies."

"Well, the Hollywood folks got it right this time. There are Apaches. Thousands of them live down in southern New Mexico."

Pablo watched closely as the man approached on horseback.

"Charlie's my only fulltime cowboy these days," Uncle Antonio said, scanning the western horizon for any signs of rain. The sky was awash in colors of red, yellow, and gold. Far to the south, perhaps forty miles away, a curtain of virga —rain that never reaches the ground—descended from a patch of dark clouds.

"Where does he sleep at night?" Pia asked.

"On the ground, Pia," Uncle Antonio said. "The Bar-7 has sixty miles of fence. It takes Charlie most of the summer to ride all of it. Once every week or so he'll return to the Bar-7 for supplies. He'll spend a few days here resting up at his place up on the mesa, then he's back riding fence."

A three-legged dog ran alongside the Apache cowboy's caramel-colored Mustang. Pablo noted that the dog was missing its right rear leg, but was making good time.

Charlie rode over to where everyone was seated on the corral fence. His weathered skin was the color of adobe and his shoulders were stooped with age. Beneath his wide-brimmed cowboy hat he wore his snow-white hair in a single braid, which stretched to the middle of his back. A single white feather was attached to the end of the braid.

"*Dago Te*, Antonio Flores," Charlie said in Apache, his voice cracking with age.

"*Dago Te*, Charlie Pecos," Uncle Antonio replied. "How goes the fence-mending business, my friend?"

Charlie reported that the barbed wire fences bordering Pasture Five had not weathered the winter and spring too well and needed mending. "I also had to dig several new fence holes," the Apache cowboy said. "The fence on the south side of Pasture Six also needed some work."

Uncle Antonio introduced his nieces and nephew to Charlie, and the Apache man gently guided his Mustang over to where they sat on the fence. He leaned over and one by one shook their hands.

"What happened to your dog, Mr. Pecos?" Pia asked, glimpsing the three-legged pooch, which had jumped into a water trough to cool off. Standing in the water up to its neck, the thirsty mutt was lapping the water.

"Coyote ate his leg when he was a pup," Charlie said, glancing down at the gray mongrel. "He's as tough as wet leather. Named him Sampson."

Pia giggled. "Sampson. That's a good name."

"I always thought so," Charlie said.

"He does just fine on three legs," Kiki observed.

"He has no idea he is handicapped," Charlie said, his gray eyes twinkling. "I don't have the heart to tell him."

"Charlie, did you see anything of those Ragland boys?" Uncle Antonio asked, placing his note pad in his shirt pocket.

"Not lately," Charlie replied. "How was the count?"

Uncle Antonio shook his head. "Not good."

Charlie fell silent.

"Kids rode up on those Raglands over near Cottonwood Ravine," Uncle Antonio said. "They had a heifer down and were butchering it."

Charlie nodded. "There is an old Indian saying: 'Stolen food never satisfies hunger.' These men will continue to steal."

"That makes three we've lost this spring," Antonio said.

"Make that four," Charlie said, holding up four fingers. "I found a carcass under the train trestle near Tortilla Flat."

"Where the tracks cross Dry Creek?"

Charlie nodded. "A pack of coyotes were under the trestle feeding on what was left of the carcass. Could have died of natural causes, but I read sign all around the carcass.

The Raglands have a pack mule. It has a bad front hoof. Leaves a crooked imprint. It was them alright."

Antonio Flores frowned and started to say something, but just then the supper bell rang.

The cowboys milling around the corral made a beeline for the ranch house. Several others poured out of the barn and across the barnyard toward the sprawling ranch house.

"Those Ragland brothers will be the death of me yet," Uncle Antonio said sadly.

Chapter 5

It was branding day at the Bar-7 ranch.

Pablo had set his bunkhouse alarm clock for five, but he and his sister and cousin were up and gone before it went off. They were the first ones to arrive at the ranch house for breakfast. Well, almost the first. Uncle Antonio and Aunt Helen were already in the kitchen. Uncle Antonio was making coffee while his wife cooked breakfast.

"Weatherman says we may get some rain later today, kids," Uncle Antonio said, always the optimist. "Sure hope so. A hundred and seventeen days without rain."

In a few minutes, the volunteer crew of Bar-7 cowboys began arriving in ones and twos in pickup trucks large and small, and the kitchen was soon bustling with activity. A few had slept over in the bunkhouse.

***

As the rosy blush of dawn filled the eastern New Mexico sky, Pablo, Pia, and Kiki followed Uncle Antonio across the barnyard to the branding corral. The air was cool and clear, and off to the west the Burro Mountains looked so close that Pablo thought he could almost reach out and touch them. Their lofty peaks rose in the distance like a stone sculpture.

Uncle Antonio said the first step in the branding process was the most difficult: separating the mother cows from their calves. It was tricky business. Each cowboy's horse was trained to separate the calf from its mother, and it required some fancy horsemanship. Pablo, Pia, and Kiki watched in amazement from the top rung of the branding corral fence awaiting their job assignments from Uncle Antonio.

Pablo marveled at the organized performance put on by the cowboys and their cutting horses. It reminded him of a well-trained military drill team. Mounted on horseback, one cowboy would rope the calf by its hind legs—that in itself was downright amazing—and then gently drag the calf to a waiting cowboy on the ground, who tied the animal's legs. A team of three other cowboys rushed in and gave the calf a shot to immunize it against disease, branded it, and then tagged its ears—the tags identified each calf.

The calves bawled for their mothers, and the handful of big bulls in a nearby corral snorted and pawed at the earth, angered by what they were hearing. The big steers were fathers to the calves, and the bawling made the bulls restless.

The branding procedure took less than a minute. Uncle Antonio told his nephew and nieces that the process had been done the same way at the Bar-7 for more than a hundred years.

"We've tried other methods," Uncle Antonio explained, "but the old-fashioned way works best."

The branding looked cruel to Pia, whose job was to tally the number of calves that were branded. The calf's thick hide smoked when the red-hot Bar-7 branding iron was pressed against it, and it was all Pia could do to watch. But Uncle Antonio eased her fears.

"Have you ever had a shot, Pia?" Uncle Antonio asked gently.

"I stepped on a nail last summer and had to have a shot," Pia said.

"Probably a tetanus shot. Did it hurt?"

"Not much."

"Well, that's about how the branding feels to these calves," he said. "Doesn't hurt much at all. Scares them more than hurts them."

Pia felt better after that.

It was Pablo's job to keep the charcoal fire going in the branding pot, which consisted of a big iron kettle that held the branding irons. It sat at one end of the branding corral.

Kiki was busy shooting pictures with her camera and taking notes on her phone.

By noon, more than one hundred and fifty calves had been branded.

***

It happened without warning.

It was lunchtime, and Pablo and his sister and cousin were walking across the barnyard toward the ranch house with their Uncle Antonio when there was a loud commotion back at the bullpen. One of the big steers—he had been pawing the earth all morning—was butting the corral fence with his head and horns, and causing quite a racket.

"He's ready for a fight," Uncle Antonio said, glancing back over his shoulder. "We'll have to keep an eye on him."

At that moment, the bull bellowed wildly, pawed the earth one last time, and then jumped the corral fence, knocking off the top rail.

Cowboys scattered, running and shouting.

"Bull's on the loose!" one of the cowhands screamed as he scampered up the branding corral fence.

"Inside the trailer, kids!" Uncle Antonio yelled, rushing into a nearby horse trailer. Pablo and Kiki were a step behind.

Once inside the trailer, Kiki shouted, "Where's Pia?"

Pablo's head snapped around, and he peered between the wooden slats of the horse trailer. What he saw made his heart stutter to a complete stop before leaping into his throat.

Frozen with fear, Pia was standing where they had left her in the middle of the barnyard, her eyes as big as silver dollars. The angry bull had spotted Pablo's sister and was charging toward her. Snorting and bellowing, the bull's big hoofs filled the air with dust. Head down, he was preparing to put his horns to work.

"PIA! RUN!" Pablo yelled at the top of his lungs.

But Pia Perez was paralyzed with fear.

Pablo started to dash out of the trailer and run to his sister's aid, but the bull was almost upon her now. He could never get to her in time. He was powerless to help.

"PIA RUN!" Kiki screamed.

But Pia was rooted to the ground.

"Oh, no," Uncle Antonio said quietly. He closed his eyes, snatched his weathered hat from his head, and clutched it to his chest.

Then, out of thin air, Charlie Pecos appeared. Mounted on his Mustang, he galloped at full speed past the corral toward Pia, his feathered braid streaming in the wind. Sampson was running alongside the Mustang, yelping furiously.

In the next moment, Sampson was on one side of the charging bull and Charlie and his muscular stallion were on the other. Sampson's loud barks diverted the bull's attention, and the one-ton animal tossed its head and bawled insanely at the three-legged mutt. The distraction gave Charlie the split-second opening he needed, and he raced past the big steer and swept up Pia with one arm and then clutched her safely to his body.

The enraged bull continued on across the barnyard and out to the open prairie.

"Thank heavens," Uncle Antonio whispered.

Pablo felt weak in his knees and he grabbed the open door of the horse trailer for support.

Uncle Antonio, Pablo, and Kiki stepped out of the trailer. Charlie brought Pia over to where they stood, setting her gently on the ground.

Pia's face was as pale as a flake of snow.

Pablo tried to speak—even to swallow—but his throat was dry. For a moment, he thought he might be sick.

Kiki had been holding her breath during the entire episode, and she gasped with a grimace, releasing all the air in her lungs.

***

"Uncle Antonio," Pablo said. "How old is Charlie Pecos?"

They were seated beside their uncle at the lunch table with the other cowboys. The table was covered with more heaping bowls of food than Pablo had ever seen: mashed potatoes, fried chicken, pork chops, corn on the cob, green beans, pitchers of buttermilk, and a couple of Mexican dishes. The cowboys were laughing and joking, and piling food onto their plates as if they hadn't eaten in days. A cowboy named Billy Soto was talking to one of the other cowboys in Spanish.

"I've heard he's seventy-five," Uncle Antonio said, drowning a pair of biscuits in brown gravy. "I've also heard he's eighty-five."

"He acts more like twenty-five," Kiki said. "The way he reached down at a full gallop and gathered up Pia was, well, unbelievable."

"I could feel my heart beating," Pia said, placing her hand over her heart.

After rescuing Pia, Charlie Pecos had vanished as quickly as he had appeared.

"How long has he worked for you?" Pablo asked.

Squinting one eye shut, Uncle Antonio looked up at the ceiling. "He's worked summers for me for as long as I can remember. Forty years, I'd guess." Uncle Antonio set the gravy bowl aside, and then said, "Forty-two years, to be exact. He worked for my father to begin with. I was no more than eight or nine at the time."

"Where does he live?" Pia asked.

"Most of the year he lives at the Mescalero Apache Indian Reservation, a hundred miles or so south of here," Uncle Antonio said. "He rides in from the reservation each spring, and rides home in the fall."

"He doesn't have a car?" Pia said, surprised.

Uncle Antonio laughed. "No, Pia, Charlie doesn't have a car. I'm sure he doesn't even know how to drive."

"I thought all adults knew how to drive," Pia said.

"Not Charlie Pecos," Pia's uncle said. "He stays in a little place up on Saddle Horn Mesa. Offered him a bed in the bunkhouse, but he'd rather stay up on the mesa. He's a quiet sort. Likes to be by himself. I respect that."

Pablo had noted Saddle Horn Mesa the first day at the ranch. It rose up from the desert floor two miles south of the ranch house. The picturesque mesa dominated the eastern landscape.

"I never got a chance to thank him," Pia said. Then, in a small voice, she added, "He saved my life, Uncle Antonio."

His eyes misty, Uncle Antonio nodded solemnly. "Yes, he did, Pia."

Most of the cowboys at the table were listening to the conversation, and they agreed with one another: Charlie Pecos had, indeed, saved Pia's life.

"Why didn't you run, Pia?" Pablo asked sharply. He was upset with his sister for nearly giving him a heart attack.

"I tried, Pablo, but my legs wouldn't work," Pia protested. "They felt rubbery. I was really scared. I'm sure glad Mr. Pecos…" Pia left the thought dangling in the air. She choked back a sob.

"We need to find Charlie Pecos and thank him," Kiki said, comforting her cousin. "That was a brave thing he did."

"You can say that again," Pablo said.

"That was a brave thing he did," Kiki teased.

Everyone laughed. The laughter helped relieve the tension they felt from reliving the frightful moment.

Chapter 6

Saddle Horn Mesa rose six hundred feet above the New Mexico prairie. The flat top of the mesa—the word "mesa" was Spanish for "table"—covered an area of about a square city block. It had been formed over millions of years as the desert around it eroded.

Pablo, Pia, and Kiki had come to Saddle Horn Mesa to thank Charlie Pecos for saving Pia's life.

The trail leading to the top of the mesa was rocky and steep. Starting at the base of the mesa, it climbed upward in a series of dizzying zigzag formations. The trail was also narrow, and they were forced to dismount and carefully walk their horses up the uneven pathway. The trail reminded Pablo of pictures he had seen of the switchback pathway leading to the bottom of the Grand Canyon.

Pia seemed more concerned about her pony's safety than she did her own, and she spoke softly to Short Stuff as they made their way up the irregular mesa trail.

"Easy, girl. Take it slow," Pia cautioned, leading Short Stuff by the reins.

The trip to the top of the mesa took half an hour.

It was a magnificent view from the summit. The faraway Burro Mountains rose into the clouds twenty miles to the west, their slopes still speckled with winter snow. At the base of the mountains was the deserted mining town of Axe Handle. It was a flyspeck in the distance.

"Quite the view," Kiki said, snapping some pictures with her camera.

Pablo immediately spotted the place Charlie Pecos called home. It wasn't much more than a small, cone-shaped hut. Long, flexible limbs had been buried in the ground and bent into arches to make a frame. Dried brush covered the frame, and an opening had been made for a doorway. The cone-shaped hut was constructed on the edge of a growth of piñon trees, fifty yards or so from where the trail spilled out onto the mesa.

Charlie's caramel-colored Mustang was grazing in a scrawny patch of grass nearby, its front legs hobbled with rope. Neither Charlie Pecos nor Sampson the Wonder Dog, however, was anywhere to be seen. (Pablo had given the dog his new name after the mutt had helped save Pia.)

"Mr. Pecos!" Pablo called out.

No answer.

"Maybe he's out hunting or looking for arrowheads or

whatever Apaches do in their spare time," Kiki said. She snapped a picture of Charlie's hut. "I can work this into my story."

"Gosh, it isn't much of a…house," Pia observed.

Pablo scanned the surrounding terrain. The mesa appeared deserted, and they walked their horses over to the entrance of the grass hut and peered inside. The Apache cowboy's possessions were meager: a bedroll, a few pots and pans, a saddlebag, a small shovel, a pair of coiled ropes, a Bible, and a couple of paperback books. Pablo could make out the title of one paperback: *Call of the Wild* by Jack London. A cooking pit had been dug a few feet outside the hut. Wisps of smoke rose from the ashes.

"Well, he couldn't be far," Pablo said, gesturing at the smoldering fire.

"Pablo, what do Apaches do in their spare time?" Pia asked.

Pablo laughed. "I guess you'll have to asked Charlie Pecos when—"

"Dago Te!"

The loud voice had come from behind them, and they whirled around to see Charlie Pecos standing ten feet away. He had appeared as if from nowhere. Wagging his tail playfully, Sampson the Wonder Dog stood beside him.

"Whew!" Kiki gasped softly. "You scared the you-know-what out of me, Mr. Pecos."

"Me...too," Pia said in a jumpy voice, one hand over her heart.

"Dago Te!" Charlie Pecos repeated, bringing his hand up in a greeting gesture.

"Dago Te!" they said, still a bit stunned by the Apache man's sudden appearance.

"I watched you ride from the ranch," Charlie Pecos said, his voice creaking with age. "I watched you climb the trail."

Pablo nodded and said, "Yes, we've come to thank you for saving—"

"What does *Dago Te* mean, Mr. Pecos?" Pia said promptly.

The Apache man smiled. "Hello."

"Dago Te!" Pia said again with a big grin.

"And a second *Dago Te*! to you, little one," Charlie Pecos replied.

"We wanted to thank you for saving Pia from that bull," Pablo said, giving Pia a sour look for interrupting him.

"That was very brave of you," Kiki said.

"There is an old Indian saying: 'The ones that matter most are the children. They are the true human beings,'" Charlie Pecos said.

"Indian?" Kiki said, grinning. "Wouldn't you rather be called Native American?"

"Nobody asked Charlie Pecos what he wanted to be called," Charlie said. "Come into my *kowa*, my home." The old man lowered his head, entered his hut and then waved them inside. They crawled inside and sat on the ground across from the Apache Indian. Sampson the Wonder Dog found a shady spot outside under a mesquite bush.

"I'm sure glad you rode by when you did, Mr. Pecos," Pia said. "That bull was mean."

"No, not mean, little one," Charlie said. "He is who is he —a bull. He longs, like we all do, to be free." He paused, and then said, "It is like my horse Moses. I must hobble him—he too, longs to be free."

"He's a fine looking animal," Kiki said, glancing out the doorway at the powerful stallion.

"I've never seen a horse run so fast," Pablo said. "Where'd you find him?"

"He is from a small Mustang herd that runs wild on the prairie west of here," Charlie said. "Sometimes he smells the herd and longs to be with them."

"How did you catch him, Mr. Pecos?" Pia asked.

Charlie Pecos felt uncomfortable at being called Mr. Pecos, and he asked them to call him Charlie. They said that they would.

"So how did you catch him, Charlie?" Pablo said. There were a thousand questions Pablo wanted to ask the Apache man.

"It wasn't me that caught him," Charlie said, a smile tugging at the corners of his withered lips. "It was a mud hole

where Dry Creek begins to climb into the Burro Mountains."
He paused. "In years past, Dry Creek wasn't always dry. As it
flows from the mountains, even today in some spots, it carries
water."

"It hasn't rained in one hundred and seventeen days,"
Kiki said soberly.

"One hundred and eighteen," Charlie said. "Another
piece of Mother Earth dies each day."

Pablo said, "You found Moses in a mud hole?"

Charlie grinned. "I was riding fence for your uncle on an
old cow pony three summers ago when I came upon Moses.
That wasn't his name at the time. That is a name I later gave
him. He was struggling mightily in the mud, but the more he
fought the mud the deeper he sank. I threw a rope around the
Mustang's neck, and the cow pony and I pulled him out.
Moses is still mad at me for capturing him," the Apache man
said. "Three years and he is still mad. I see in my mind the
day I will set him free, but until then, he must be my legs."

"Well, I'm just glad you happened by when you did,"
Pablo said. "There was no stopping that bull."

Charlie chuckled. "I sometimes see things from afar in
my mind. It is a gift."

No one spoke. Pablo and Kiki glanced at each other out
the corners of their eyes.

Somewhere on the mesa a crow cawed. A moment later,
a second crow answered.

"You mean your...eyesight is good?" Kiki asked hesitantly.

"Oh, yes, my eyesight is excellent, but my mind is also excellent. I sometimes see faraway people and places in my mind. It is a gift from God."

"You knew the bull was going to escape?" Pia said, trying to make sense of it.

"I was inside the barn feeding Moses when the bull jumped the fence. I saw him in my mind," the Mescalero Apache explained. Looking at Pia, he said, "I saw you frozen with fear. I saw the bull charging toward you."

"Oh," Pia said softly, sneaking a glance at her older brother.

"The bull was very angry that his sons and daughters were being branded," Charlie said. "He could not stand to see the brands being made, and his children suffering. He wanted away from that place. He wanted to be free from the suffering of his children."

"But Uncle Antonio said the branding doesn't hurt the calves," Pia said.

Charlie smiled. "Yes, but the bull doesn't know that."

Again, there was a long pause.

Pablo and Kiki shared another quick sideways glance, and then Kiki said, "You see things...things from afar, Charlie? Do I have that right? You actually see...things?"

Charlie Pecos nodded. "It is a gift."

Pronouncing each word slowly, Pablo said, "That's interesting."

They sat talking for the longest time to Charlie Pecos. It filled Pablo with a warm feeling. Talking to a real Indian. Although Pablo wasn't a hundred percent convinced the Apache man could see things from afar, it didn't matter. There was something about the man that gave Pablo total peace.

***

An hour or so into the conversation, Kiki asked Charlie Pecos about his home on the Mescalero Reservation, but the Apache cowboy had fallen asleep in a sitting position. His chin rested against his chest. They tiptoed silently out of his hut and walked their horses quietly to the trail leading down from the mesa. They paused briefly at the trailhead.

"Charlie Pecos is awesome," Pablo said. "I'm not sure what to make of his gift. It's hard to understand how—"

"Pablo!" Kiki cried. "Look!" She pointed in the direction of the Burro Mountains.

Pablo peered into the clear New Mexico sky. "What? I don't see anything."

"I do," Pia cried, raising her hand and leveling a finger toward the distant mountains.

When Pablo looked a second time he saw something,

but it didn't register at first. "It's a bird," Pablo said. "A...big bird. Isn't it?"

"Yeah, it's a bird alright!" Kiki said. "And if I'm not mistaken, it's a bird with spinning blades on top! Get your binoculars!"

Pablo plucked his 8X binoculars from his saddlebag and immediately brought them up to his eyes.

"Is it a helicopter, Pablo?" Pia said.

Pablo focused the binoculars and then nodded. "Yeah, Pia, it is. It looks like they're chasing a herd of antelope." Clouds of dust twirled into the air behind the frightened animals. Pablo could even make out the writing on the side of the sleek aircraft: **Bell 407**. "It says Bell four zero seven on the side. Its landing skids are about ten feet long."

"Skids? Hello!" Kiki exclaimed, remembering the skid-like impressions in the sand not far from the mouth of Petroglyph Canyon.

The petroglyphs might be in danger again, Pablo thought, and he quickly ran some numbers through his head: Half an hour to get down from the mesa. Another half-hour (maybe less) to reach the ranch house. Still another hour to reach the canyon. It might take them two hours to ride to the canyon. However, if he rode by himself—Buster was much faster than Queen Mary or Short Stuff—he might make it in an hour and a half.

Maybe less.

Pablo looked squarely at Kiki. "I want you and Pia to go back to the ranch. Once these helicopter clowns have had their fun with the antelope, they'll head toward the canyon, and I plan to catch them in the act of stealing the glyphs. I'll meet you at the ranch later."

"As if!" Kiki snapped.

"Yeah, Pablo," Pia said. "As if!"

"I don't have time to argue." Reins in hand, Pablo walked the big brown and white Paint named Buster onto the rocky trail leading down from the mesa.

Pablo deliberately took it slow down the mesa trail. He didn't want to endanger his sister and cousin. It would be different when the perilous zigzag trail was behind them, and when Pablo reached the desert floor, he immediately swung up into the saddle and gave Buster a nudge—the stallion broke into a gallop. When Pablo looked back over his shoulder, Pia and Kiki were falling behind. A minute later, he was far ahead.

He had to get to the canyon. The sooner the better.

Chapter 7

His sinister diversion at an end—the antelope were getting smarter and it was becoming harder and harder to chase them over the rim and into Petroglyph Canyon—Truman Hathaway flew south along the magnificent gorge, and in a few minutes the Bell 407 landed on the uneven lip of Petroglyph Canyon.

"This is where you get out," Hathaway told Pirate.

"Gladly," Pirate said, unbuckling his seatbelt.

"Got your walkie-talkie?" Red asked.

"Does it look like I got my walkie-talkie?" Pirate said, grasping the two-way radio in his hand.

"Use it," Hathaway said. "I don't want to find myself staring down the barrel of Sheriff Frost's—"

"I'll use it," Pirate said promptly.

"And don't be drawing them pictures when ya oughta be watching," Red warned. "No pictures!"

"I done heard you the first time. No pictures," Pirate replied.

"Good! Now git!" Red ordered.

Pirate climbed out of the helicopter, the walkie-talkie tucked under his arm. The main rotor blade was still spinning and he ducked his head until he was a safe distance from the chopper.

From this spot Pirate had a grand view of Petroglyph Canyon and the dry riverbed leading to it. Indeed, he could see someone approaching from any direction ten minutes before they reached the mouth of the wilderness gorge.

The turbine engine roared, and the sleek, six-passenger aircraft lifted off.

Pirate waited until the helicopter was out of sight before walking over to a large, flat rock. He lifted one end of the rock, thrust his hand under it, and removed a pad and pencil hidden there. He sat on the rock and began sketching a distant cloud formation. A dark curtain of virga hung from the puffy clouds.

***

Framed on either side by the steep canyon walls—the canyon provided good cover—the Bell 407 flew south until it reached the narrow throat of the gorge. Proceeding slowly through the narrow entrance, the helicopter flew over Dry Creek and landed not far from *Arbol Grande*.

"Okay, boys," Hathaway said, "make it fast."

Red and Gordo hurriedly climbed out of the helicopter

with their gear. Red carried a six-foot crowbar, a small aluminum ladder, and a walkie-talkie. Gordo had a chainsaw in one hand and a gunnysack in the other. Each man had a canteen attached to his belt. They headed straight for the canyon entrance.

Gordo's chainsaw was nothing more than a modified logger's chainsaw. He had replaced the original steel cutting chain with one made of carbon steel, described by many as the hardest metal in the world. The carbon-steel blade could slice through sandstone rock like a hot knife through butter. The saw weighed less than twenty-five pounds. Inside Gordo's gunnysack were a half a dozen cheap bath towels they would use to wrap each valuable glyph.

The two brothers hurried across Dry Creek and into the mouth of the canyon. Two minutes later they were standing before a Mother Rock decorated with a multitude of pristine petroglyphs. There was little circulation of air in the box canyon—it was blowtorch hot—and sweat rolled down the faces of both men.

Gordo paused to catch his breath (he was hopelessly out of shape) and then gave the starter cord a tug. The lightweight gasoline engine buzzed to life on the first pull.

Red stepped over to the Mother Rock and laid his hand on a primitive rock drawing of a deer and its fawn, a beautiful glyph. He gave his brother the thumbs up, and Gordo moved in with his saw.

Gordo was becoming skilled at extracting the rock art. In the beginning he had destroyed as many as he had successfully removed, but he was more experienced now and in a few short minutes he had made five surgical incisions around the pristine glyph. He turned the engine off, set the rock saw in the sand, and then took another big drink from his canteen.

"Good work, bro," Red said, setting the ladder against the Mother Rock. When Gordo started to mount the ladder, Red said: "Hold up a minute." He punched the SEND button on his walkie-talkie and said, "Pirate, ya see anything?"

There were a few moments of silence, and then Pirate reported, "Not a thing. Coast is clear."

"Ya ain't drawing pictures, are ya?" Red yapped.

"No, I ain't drawing pictures!" came Pirate's offended reply.

Red set the walkie-talkie aside and gave Gordo the sign to continue.

Gordo wiped his forehead with the sleeve of his shirt, and with some difficulty climbed up and onto the third rung of the ladder. From there he had a better angle to make the sixth and final incision. He pulled the cord. The engine roared to life immediately, and he quickly made the sixth cut.

Red hurriedly wedged one end of his crowbar into five of the six incisions, pressing lightly on the end of the crowbar each time. He then traded places with Gordo on the ladder and gently inserted the end of the iron bar into the sixth incision. Red leaned on his crowbar lightly, and the 3,000-year-old rock drawing made a soft snapping sound and separated from the Mother Rock in one piece.

"Bingo!" Red crowed happily.

Gordo grabbed the rock drawing as it slid down the face of the Mother Rock.

During the next fifteen minutes Red Ragland and his behemoth brother excavated six more rock drawings: a ten-pointed asterisk; a long-necked bird, wings extended; a coyote-like creature, mouth open, tail outstretched; three tiny squares stacked together; a geometric figure of stairs; and two small side-by-side circles connected by a straight line. Carefully wrapping each glyph in a bath towel, the rock drawings were then placed into the gunnysack The glyph total should have been seven, but the sandstone Mother Rock was fighting back and had pinched Gordo's saw blade. The only way Gordo could pull the blade free was to crack the glyph into a dozen pieces with the crowbar. Better to lose the glyph than the carbon-steel saw blade. Besides, there were hundreds of other glyphs in the canyon.

***

Pia and Kiki arrived at the canyon just as Pablo emerged from the narrow entrance an hour later. Buster was tied nearby to *Arbol Grande*.

They rode over to him.

"Were they here?" Kiki said in an excited voice.

Before Pablo could answer, Pia said, "Why didn't you wait for us, Pablo?"

"I thought it might be dangerous, Pia," Pablo replied. "Besides, I knew the looters wouldn't be here very long, and I wanted to catch them in the act."

"And how exactly had you planned on catching them in the act?" Kiki said in a mocking tone of voice. "What was your plan, Sherlock?"

"Yeah, Pablo Perez," Pia scolded, "what was your plan?"

He looked up at his sister and cousin with an embarrassed grin. "Actually, I, uh, didn't really have a plan. I thought maybe I could duck down beside some rocks and take a picture—"

"What about Buster?" Pia said, still unhappy about being left behind. "What were you going to do with Buster if the looters were here? They'd see him."

"Like I said, I didn't really have a plan."

"It's probably a good thing they were gone," Kiki said. "I don't think the Ragland brothers, or whoever is stealing the glyphs, would take kindly to having their pictures taken in the act of looting."

Pablo nodded.

"And another thing," Kiki pointed out, "that helicopter may have been, gosh, I don't know, a television news helicopter from Albuquerque. So we don't even know the looters were here."

"Oh, they were here, alright," Pablo said.

"How do you know, Pablo?" Pia asked.

"Several more glyphs were carved out," he noted sadly. "And they destroyed another one. There was nothing left but pieces on the ground." He dug the pieces out of his pocket and cradled what remained of the dismembered rock art in his hands.

"That makes me so mad," Kiki said, sneering.

"You've got to take their picture, Pablo!" Pia cried.

***

"Pablo, do you believe that Charlie Pecos has a, you know…a gift from God?" Pia asked. She had a puzzled look on her face.

Seated in the shade of *Arbo Grande,* they were allowing their horses to rest before returning to the ranch.

"I suppose it's possible," Pablo replied. "There's a lot about the world we can't comprehend."

"It's like Uncle Antonio said about the petroglyphs," Kiki said. "People can't read them because they haven't been decoded. Same goes for Charlie. Maybe it's a God-given gift that works in ways we simply don't understand."

"I think it's real," Pia said confidently.

"He saved Pia," Kiki observed. "He said he was in the

barn, but saw the bull jumping the fence in his mind. He saw Pia rooted in place. What did you just say, Pablo? There is a lot about the world we don't understand."

Pablo nodded tentatively.

"Actually," Kiki said, "there is a name for what Charlie can do, or says he can do."

"There is?" Pablo asked, his eyebrows drawn together.

"I can't remember what it's called exactly, but I'll bet I can find out." Kiki pulled out here phone and immediately accessed the Internet. She had service. "Let's do a search."

"If you don't know what it's called, how can you do a search?" Pia said.

"It has something to do with being psychic."

"What's that?" Pia said, frowning.

"Sort of like ESP," Pablo said. "And if you ask me what ESP is I'm going to have a heat stroke."

"I know what ESP is...sort of."

"I'll start by searching the word 'psychic' on Google." Kiki's fingers danced over the tiny screen. In a moment, she grimaced. "Gosh, only sixty million websites for the word 'psychic.'"

"Try psychic powers," Pablo suggested.

Kiki typed in the new search words, and waited a few moments. "Ah, perfect! The Top Ten Psychic Powers is the first site. Maybe that will tell us something."

"Yeah, go there," Pablo said eagerly.

Kiki went to the site, enlarged the screen and began to hurriedly read the listings for The Top Ten Psychic Powers.

"Number one is Channeling," Kiki said. She laughed softly. "I don't even know what Channeling is."

"Me neither," Pablo said.

"Two is Clairvoyance…"

"I've heard of that," Pablo said.

"Not that either. Three is Dowsing. You know. Finding water. Nope. Four is ESP. Nay. Five is Medical Intuition. No. Six is Psychometry…"

"What the heck's that?" Pablo said.

Kiki read the definition: "'Psychometry is a person's ability to gather information from the energy of objects, photographs, or places.'"

"If you say so," Pablo said.

"It's possible," Kiki insisted. "Anything's possible."

"Okay, it's possible," Pablo said in a guarded voice.

Kiki turned back to the website, her eyes widening. "Yes!" she explained. "Number eight is Remote Viewing!" She looked at Pablo and Pia. "That's it! That's what it's called!"

Pablo appeared skeptical. "What does it say about remote viewing?" He had never heard the term.

Kiki began reading:

"'Remote Viewing is the ability of a person to gather information on a remote location that is hidden from the physical sight of the viewer and is separated from the viewer by some distance, often thousands of miles. It is a form of extra-sensory perception. The U.S. Central Intelligence Agency has experimented with this psychic phenomenon for many years with varying degrees of success.'"

Kiki looked up. "Hey, if it's good enough for the CIA, it's good enough for me!"

Pablo laughed.

"So," Pia said, "it's true? Charlie has this remote viewing thing?"

Kiki offered a shrug. "Maybe."

They mounted up and headed back toward the ranch. The afternoon heat rose up from Dry Creek in shimmering waves. Thunder mumbled and groaned somewhere in the distance.

Chapter 8

"You kids are welcome to tag along," Uncle Antonio said at breakfast the following morning. The gathering was over, and all the calves had been branded. The final count was two hundred and eighteen, far below what had been expected. The ranch couldn't operate on the money from only two hundred and eighteen calves, and Uncle Antonio was headed to the bank in Santa Fe to ask for a loan.

"There's plenty of things to do and see in Santa Fe," Uncle Antonio said. "You kids might enjoy a day out of the saddle. And here's the really good part…"

Pia couldn't wait for the answer. "What, Uncle Antonio?" she asked excitedly.

"You won't run into the Ragland brothers."

"Oh, Uncle Antonio," Pia said, "I thought it was something really special." She put on a hurt face.

"That's special enough, Pia," her uncle cheered. "Or maybe you'd rather run down some yearlings from the back of Short Stuff?" A big grin stretched his tan-colored face.

"No, thanks," Pia replied. "My bum is still sore." She smothered her pancakes with Aunt Helen's homemade concoction of honey and syrup.

"And my legs are permanently bowed," Pablo complained with a smile.

"The life of a cowboy isn't easy," Uncle Antonio said, sipping his coffee. "Never was, probably never will be." He cast a sober glance at Helen. "Don't know how long I'll be at the bank, kids. Maybe an hour. Maybe longer."

Pablo noted an odd, troubled expression on his Aunt Helen's face. Her lips were pursed and she was nervously twisting one end of her apron into a knot.

"One hundred and nineteen days without rain," Helen Flores said in a tired voice. She removed the pot of coffee from the wood-burning stove, stepped around the table to where her husband was seated, and then refilled his mug. "Worst drought ever."

Uncle Antonio looked up at his wife, a sorrowful cast to his dark brown eyes. "It'll be okay, Helen. Things will work out fine. Mr. Kenney will be here about noon with his livestock trailers. He and his men will have the calves loaded up and out of here by three—four at the latest. He'll leave you a check."

"Where are the calves going, Uncle Antonio?" Pia asked.

"Have to sell them, Pia," he replied. "Pure and simple.

Don't want to. I'd like to let them grow a bit before I send them off to market, but there just isn't enough grass for them to eat. Can't afford hay." He rubbed the stubble on his chin and shook his head like a man troubled by circumstances. "Calves this year were sixty pounds lighter than last year. Skinny little critters and not nearly enough of them. We gathered more than four hundred last year." He removed his glasses and cleaned them with the sleeve of his shirt. "A hundred and nineteen days without rain," he said quietly.

"Worst drought ever," Helen sighed.

***

Uncle Antonio parked his Ford pickup at a public lot a block south of the Santa Fe Plaza, and everyone piled out.

"I have your cell number, Kiki," Uncle Antonio said, looking in the truck's side mirror and straightening his tie. He was wearing a dark suit and black cowboy boots. He ran a callused hand over his hair, straightening it the best he could. "I'll give you kids a call when I'm ready to leave the bank. We'll meet somewhere in town." He flashed a big grin. "Maybe get some ice cream."

"Ice creams sounds good," Pia beamed.

Uncle Antonio made one final adjustment to his tie. "I read something about a parade today here in Santa Fe. Maybe you kids would enjoy watching it." He gestured at the camera attached to Kiki's belt. "Might make for some dandy pictures."

They walked together as far as the intersection of Santa Fe Trail and San Francisco Street, then Uncle Antonio headed one way and his nephew and nieces another.

Kiki picked up a newspaper called the *Santa Fe Scene* from a newspaper rack on the plaza. The newspaper was free. She said the newspaper might have details about the parade, and they found an empty bench in the plaza and leafed through it.

The Santa Fe Plaza was a square block of trees, grass, and red brick sidewalks. A forty-foot-tall monument commemorating an important Civil War battle formed the plaza centerpiece. While Pablo and Kiki thumbed through the newspaper, Pia strolled over to the monument and read the brass inscription at the base of the tall column.

There wasn't much to be found about the parade in the newspaper, and they decided to investigate the downtown area, which was bursting at the seams with tourists dressed in brightly colored shirts and walking shorts. Most of them had cameras draped around their necks.

The north side of the Plaza was a marketplace for Native Americans wearing Nike T-shirts; they sold their arts and crafts from blankets spread out on the sidewalk. Pablo, Pia, and Kiki spent nearly half an hour inspecting the colorful array of arts and crafts, including turquoise jewelry, delicately painted ceramic pots, and hand-woven blankets. Kiki bought silver bracelets for herself and Pia. Pablo didn't find anything that he couldn't live without.

They wandered down San Francisco Street. A sign in the window of a store called the Running Tree Art Gallery grabbed their attention. It read:

AUTHENTIC PETROGLYPHS.

"That looks interesting," Pablo said, gesturing at the sign.

"Absolutely," Kiki replied.

They went inside.

The Running Tree Art Gallery carried an assortment of well-crafted Native American goods, but Pablo thought some of the merchandise resembled the kind of trinkets a person might find in a gumball machine. There were, however, a good selection of Native American crafts such as Rio Grande blankets, pottery, turquoise, and leather belts.

And, like the window sign boasted, there was also a limited selection of petroglyphs. **PARTIALS ONLY**, another sign read.

Each of a dozen or so of the incomplete glyphs were displayed in tiny velvet chests that were lined up on a wooden shelve. Each chest lid was open, and each glyph had been named. The names were printed on white labels and attached to the lids: Morning Sun, Man With Spear, Two Circles, The Hunter.

A sign read:

IF YOU WANT TO EXAMINE A PETROGLYPH ASK THE CLERK FOR ASSISTANCE.

Not a single piece of rock art was whole. Each had a piece missing. A Bird-Headed Human with no head; a Mountain Sheep with two legs gone; a Shaman, the right side of his body absent; Concentric Circles, which Pablo thought should have been labeled Concentric Half-Circles.

A handprint called Half a Hand immediately grabbed their attention. It was missing two fingers. Pablo and Kiki peered at the piece of rock art, and then looked at one another, an undeclared awakening passing between them.

"Hey!" Pia squawked, her eyes fixed on Half a Hand. "That's the other part of—"

"Shhh!" Pablo quickly raised a finger and put it to his lips. "Don't say anything, Pia," he said in a low voice, a rush of adrenaline flooding his veins.

"That sucks, Pablo!"

"It's okay. Just chill for a minute."

Kiki called a clerk over and asked if she could examine Half a Hand.

"It's quite a fine piece of Native American art," the young man in dreadlocks said. He reminded Pablo of a famous rapper. He couldn't remember the rapper's name. "It would sell for thousands if it were in one piece."

"What are you asking for it?" Kiki asked.

"I'll have to check with the owner," the clerk said, gently removing the petroglyph from the tiny velvet chest. "We receive rock art every week and I never know the prices." He carefully laid the glyph on the counter. "You can examine it, but please don't pick it up. It's very fragile." A wide grin stretched his lips. "You break it. You buy it."

"But it's already broken," Pablo observed.

"Yes, it is," the clerk said with a diplomatic smile.

Pablo looked at his sister. "Do you have Mrs. Two Fingers?"

Pia nodded.

"Lay her on the counter, Pia."

Pia dipped her hand into the pocket of her shorts and removed the partial glyph. She laid Mrs. Two Fingers on the counter top next to Half a Hand. It was a perfect fit.

"Goodness," the young man said, looking at the two pieces, his eyes widening, "where'd that come from? It almost looks like a…a match."

"It is a match, dude," Kiki said. "A perfect match."

"I'm not sure I understand." The clerk looked confused.

"Maybe we'd better talk to the owner," Pablo said.

"I'm the assistant manager," he said. "Amadi Jones at your service. I can answer any of your questions."

"Okay, fine, Amadi," Kiki began. "Where did your glyph come from?"

Amadi paused for a moment, thinking, and then said, "Actually, I can't answer that question." He flashed an embarrassed smile.

"Can't or won't?" Pablo said.

"Can't. I just started working here last week. I'm here for the summer and—"

"So let us talk to someone who can," Kiki said in her best adult voice.

Amadi turned and disappeared through a doorway that led into the back of the shop, his lengthy dreadlocks bouncing gracefully as he walked. In a few moments, the owner appeared.

A woman in her late fifties, the heavyset gallery owner marched over to them. "I'm the gallery owner, Ginger Gideon," the woman declared. "How can I help you?"

"Look at this," Pablo said, fitting Pia's Mrs. Two Fingers with the gallery's Half a Hand to make a complete handprint glyph.

"I don't understand," the woman said, her eyes fixed on the two pieces of rock art.

"This petroglyph belongs to my sister," Pablo said, touching Mrs. Two Fingers. "We found it in a place called Petroglyph Canyon. It's a perfect fit with your glyph."

"And I should give a hoot?" Ginger said sarcastically.

"Yes, you should give a hoot," Kiki shot back, "because your half of this rare piece of Native American art has been stolen."

The storeowner smiled. "I don't think so, sister."

"I'm not your sister," Kiki replied promptly.

"We recovered our glyph from a desert canyon about fifty miles from here," Pablo said. "We had permission from the land owner to be there."

"Where did your glyph came from?" Kiki asked firmly. "And did you have permission from the land owner to be there?"

"I'll bet you didn't!" Pia snarled.

"What are you implying?" Ginger huffed, the corners of her mouth curling into a snarl. "Shouldn't you kids be with your parents?"

"We're implying that you stole this petroglyph," Kiki said. "Do you deny it?"

"Now, wait just a minute," the storeowner said, stepping back, her face suddenly boiling with anger. "You can't come into my gallery and start accusing me of—"

"So you do deny it?" Kiki asked.

"I think you little juvenile delinquents should leave," Ginger said. "Now!"

"You stole the other half of Mrs. Two Fingers!" Pia said in a loud voice.

In a hushed tone, the woman looked at Pia and said, "Keep your voice down, you little urchin."

"I'm not an urchin!" Pia squealed loudly.

"Please, keep your voice down!" Ginger repeated in a very deliberate tone, looking around the store. Several gallery customers seemed interested in the conversation. They were peering over at them.

Kiki pulled out her phone. "I'm calling the police, Miss Gideon. You're selling stolen merchandise, and I'm sure the Santa Fe police would be interested in knowing the whole story."

Ginger cleared her throat, and in a calm voice said, "I think we need to go into my office and discuss this further." She glanced for a second time at her other customers. She presented a friendly everything-is-okay smile, and then hurriedly gathered up her half of the sandstone petroglyph. "Follow me." Ginger did a quick about-face.

Pia scooped up Mrs. Two Fingers and dropped the glyph into her pocket, and Kiki stowed her phone.

They followed the storeowner into her office at the rear of the gallery. It was a small room, cluttered with papers and boxes. An Ansel Adams black and white photograph hung on the wall over Ginger's desk.

"I don't know who you think you are," Ginger growled, looking at each of them, "but the Running Tree Art Gallery is a respectable operation, and I resent the sly remark that we may have come by our rock art illegally."

"So where'd it come from?" Pablo asked, a swell of anger building inside him. The thought of someone cutting the petroglyph out of the Mother Rock was just wrong. Terribly wrong. "Or should I say, who sold it to you? We know where it came from."

"Yeah," Pia sneered, "we know where it came from."

Ginger looked squarely at Pia. "Who *are* you?"

"I'm Pia Perez from Jamesville." Pia tried to stand taller than her four-foot five-inches.

"And you think you know where my partial glyph came from?"

"Yes, I do!" Pia declared.

"Oh, really? And where might that be?" Ginger's eyes flickered nervously.

"From my Uncle Antonio's ranch, that's where!"

Ginger hesitated, and then looked at Pablo and Kiki. "We purchased the piece from one of our vendors, a respected company that has been here in Santa Fe for quite some time. We've done business with them for the past year. They're quite reputable."

"They? Who are they?" Kiki asked.

Ginger looked at each of them. "Do your parents know where you are?"

Kiki locked eyes with Ginger. "Our parents know

exactly where we are, and we know exactly where your Half a Hand came from, and I would bet that neither you nor any of your employees had the permission from the land owner to search for rock art."

"This is ruining my day," Ginger complained, opening her desk drawer. She removed a vial of pills and took one. "I have high blood pressure, and you kids are making it worse."

"And you ruined our Uncle Antonio's day," Kiki said, pulling out her phone again and dialing a number. In a moment, she said, "Operator, please give me the number for the—"

"Wait!" Ginger said, holding up her hands in a consoling gesture. "I'll tell you what you want to know if you promise to leave my store and never come back." She had been standing, but now she sighed deeply and plopped down in the chair behind her desk. It buckled under her weight. "Please don't get the police involved in this."

Kiki stowed her phone again.

"I'm guessing all your rock art came from Petroglyph Canyon," Pablo said.

"I don't know where it came from," Ginger replied, looking at Pablo. "That's the God's truth. I...do...not... know. It could have come from China for all I know. The Chinese, by the way, are very good at replicating Native American arts and crafts." She breathed another heavy sigh. "I do not know where my Half a Hand came from."

"Nor do you care, right?" Kiki said.

Ginger started to reply, thought better of it, and then cleared a place on her desk. She laid her Half a Hand on the cleared space. "May I see your piece again?" she asked Pia.

Pia looked at the woman for a long moment. "I want it back."

"You'll get it back," Ginger replied, the sting gone from her voice.

"Are you just saying that or do you really mean it?"

"Yes, yes. I really mean it."

Pia handed Mrs. Two Fingers to the woman.

The Santa Fe storeowner carefully joined the two pieces of sandstone together. "It's certainly the same piece of rock art." She looked confused.

"Your piece, unfortunately, was stolen," Pablo said.

Ginger looked up at her young agitators. "Listen, kids, I cannot be expected to monitor the origin of every piece of merchandise in my store," she said. "We have more than a hundred vendors who provide us with all sorts of original pieces of merchandise, everything from Native American moccasins to landscape pencil drawings. And if you think I'm making money hand over fist you would be gravely mistaken. I'm so far in debt it will take an Independence-Day-miracle to save me. Do you have any idea what the mortality rate is for Santa Fe businesses?"

Pablo started to respond, but Ginger had a story to tell and she would not be interrupted.

"No, you don't know. You're children. Well, I'll tell you. It's way up there. Running a retail store in Santa Fe, New Mexico, sounds very romantic, but I can tell you it is not romantic. It is a nightmare. If I had it to do all over again I'd take my husband's life-insurance money and buy a condo in Ft. Myers, Florida."

No one spoke for several long seconds.

Finally, Ginger said, "I buy all of my rock art—all of the genuine pieces, and I assume this is genuine—from a gentleman here in Santa Fe," she said. "No complete pieces. He keeps all the good pieces, the whole pieces, for himself. I always get partials...broken, chipped. We do sell whole pieces of rock art, but they're labeled as imitations."

"China?" Pablo asked.

"China," Ginger said.

"So who is this Santa Fe gentleman?" Kiki asked.

"I would hate to lose him as a vendor, and if it ever got back to him that I had told anyone about..." Her expression suddenly grew tense. "I've heard he can be, well, uh, ruthless, for lack of a better word. Last week I asked him if he could give me a break on the price, and you would have thought I had insulted his mother. He tore into me..." Ginger sighed. "I'd like to stay on his good side, if you know what I mean."

"Our lips are sealed," Pablo said. "You have our word."

"Yeah, our lips are sealed," Pia said, running her hand across her lips as if to zip them.

Cute, Pia, Pablo thought, rolling his eyes.

"The man's name is Truman Hathaway. He owns a gallery here in Santa Fe. A real art gallery. It's called Hathaway's Fine Art Gallery."

"How much do you sell your partial glyphs for?" Kiki asked.

"Does it matter?" Ginger Gideon asked.

"Not really. I'm just curious."

"The price is always negotiable. Depends on the customer," Ginger said. "I start at three hundred and work my way down. I can usually get two-fifty for each piece. My cost is a hundred, and like I said, Mr. Hathaway won't come down on his price."

"That's a pretty good profit," Kiki observed.

"No offense, dearie," Ginger said with a sarcastic grin, "but what would you know about profit or loss or anything else about business?"

"My father's a businessman back in Missouri," Kiki retorted. "I know a little about running a business."

"Listen," Ginger continued, "the truth be known, a partial glyph isn't worth squat. But Ma and Pa Kettle don't know that. Even though it may be a partial, it's an authentic petroglyph, and they're willing to shell out what I ask. Plus, each glyph comes with a certificate of authenticity."

"Are the certificates of authenticity real?" Pablo said.

Ginger laughed. "Here's the irony. The certificates are fake, but the glyphs are real."

"Yeah, irony," Pablo said gloomily.

"Like I said, kids, if I had it to do all over again, I'd be sitting in Ft. Myers right now sipping a Bloody Mary."

Pablo thanked Ginger Gideon for her time, and the three of them left the gallery and headed back toward the plaza. They paused at a stoplight waiting to cross Santa Fe Trail when Pia looked up at her older brother. "Pablo," she began, "what's an urchin?"

Chapter 9

Truman Hathaway stood in the Receiving Room of Hathaway's Fine Art Gallery admiring one of the latest additions to his collection of petroglyphs. This particular glyph was a beautiful specimen of a butterfly with its wings spread. It was from the Late Archaic period, perhaps two thousand years old. The rock drawing showed great craftsmanship. It was a true work of art, and Hathaway decided he would ask $12,000 for the uncommon glyph, but settle for $11,000. He would call it simply: The Butterfly.

Hathaway was a thin little man with dark eyes that bulged from their sockets. His face was bony and gaunt, and his jaw came to a point. The centerpiece of his attire was a tattered leather jacket, one adorned with aviation patches. He wore it day or night, for all occasions and for all seasons. He was convinced the jacket made him appear more masculine, and what's more, it was Santa Fe chic.

Hathaway's Fine Arts Gallery was one of several dozen such art showrooms bordering either side of Santa Fe's exclusive Canyon Road. If a customer expected to find something inexpensive at Hathaway's they were in the wrong place. Hathaway represented some of the best Southwest artists, including Manuel Oliva, Alex Lipe, and Gloria Kidder. Prices for their work started in the $10,000 range and went up. Other Hathaway merchandise included Navajo pottery, Zuni Fetishes, marble sculptures, etchings, and a few signed prints.

But during the past several months, Hathaway had developed an interest in petroglyphs. They commanded expensive prices, they were extremely popular with his wealthy customers, and his supply seemed to be endless.

Yes, the future was in petroglyphs.

When Susan DeCell, his sales manager, poked her head into the Receiving Room requesting Hathaway's help out on the floor, he carefully placed The Butterfly into a cloth-lined drawer of his vault, and then gently closed the heavy door. He gave the antique combination lock a couple of spins.

"What is it, Susan?" Hathaway asked, walking over to her.

"Three kids," she replied quietly. "They're interested in our petroglyphs. They wanted to speak to the owner."

"Where are their parents?"

Susan shrugged. "Don't know."

"Is this really necessary? I don't have time for a bunch of brat kids."

"They're persistent," Susan said. "They won't talk to anyone except the owner."

Hathaway uttered a dismissive groan. His time was too valuable to waste on kids. Nonetheless, he walked out of the Receiving Room and onto the merchandising floor where Pablo, Pia, and Kiki stood beside a glass counter filled with half a dozen stunning petroglyphs.

"I'm Truman Hathaway, the owner," Hathaway said, smiling around a set of teeth that were much too big for his mouth. "How can I help you children?"

Hathaway's voice had a slow, plodding quality to it. It was the kind of voice Pablo would expect to hear in a bad dream.

"Hi," Pablo said pleasantly, "I'm Pablo Perez, and this is my sister Pia and our cousin Kiki. We're from Missouri."

"Are you with your parents?" Hathaway asked in a pleasant tone of voice.

"No, we're not," Kiki replied. "We're here on vacation."

"I know you're busy, Mr. Hathaway, but could you tell us a little about this piece?" Pablo said politely, tapping the glass counter with his finger.

Pablo had tapped the glass counter above a glyph of a buffalo with two spears penetrating its side. The stunning rock art was about the size of a dinner plate. A fancy tag next to the glyph read in beautiful, gold cursive writing: Death of a Bison. To Pablo, it resembled the glyph Uncle Antonio had described, a glyph that had been stolen, a glyph of a buffalo with two spears in its side. Pablo was certain it was the same glyph that Uncle Antonio had named: Barbed Buffalo.

I know it's the same glyph, Pablo thought, his anger building.

"What would you like to know?" Hathaway glanced over at his two other customers, an African-American couple. They were inspecting an original Thomas Creed landscape painting.

"Where did it originate?" Kiki asked cordially. "It looks very southwest. Is it from this part of the country?"

"Our suppliers are located all around the world," Hathaway said in a very businesslike voice. "I would have to check our records to determine where this particular piece originated."

"What about this one?" Kiki said, indicating a rock drawing of three circles. It was labeled Circles of Wisdom.

"What's it suppose to represent?" Pablo said, trying to keep the conversation alive and fishing for answers to anything that might give them a clue about where (and how) Truman Hathaway's petroglyphs had been acquired. For all Pablo knew, Ginger Gideon had lied to them. Maybe she made up the whole story about buying partial rock drawings from Truman Hathaway. Maybe Death of a Bison was just a coincidence. Maybe there were dozens of petroglyphs of a buffalo with two spears sticking out of it. Maybe that was a popular Native American rock-art theme a few thousand years ago.

But I don't think so, Pablo thought.

"Well, young man, that is the mystery behind the piece," Hathaway said. "No one knows for certain what the creator of the piece was trying to say. It's an abstract, much like modern art."

"What's an abstract?" Pia asked, wrinkling her nose.

"Well, little lady," Hathaway said, "an abstract is something that represents an idea, not a thing."

"Oh."

"Just as French Impressionists of the late nineteenth century developed styles that were different from the styles of Surrealists of the twentieth century, so too are rock art styles different from one another." Hathaway flashed a snobby grin. He enjoyed showing off his knowledge of art. "This particular piece was created by the early inhabitants of New Mexico. Its age has been placed at five thousand B.C."

"So," Kiki asked promptly, "you do know where it originated?"

Hathaway smiled awkwardly. "Yes, I suppose I do."

Little beads of sweat had gathered beneath the swath of hair Hathaway had neatly combed over the middle of his balding skull. It was starting to run down his forehead.

"Five thousand B.C.," Pablo said. "That would make it seven thousand years old."

"Yes, young man, that would make it seven thousand years old," Hathaway said. "Now, unless you children are serious about buying one of my petroglyphs, you'll have to excuse me. I have other customers." He glanced at his two African-American customers. They were still examining the Thomas Creed painting.

Hathaway started to turn and leave when Kiki said, "That seems like a lot of money." Her eyes were fixed a small price tag lying beside Death of a Bison. It read: $13,000.

"Yes, well, authentic petroglyphs are rare these days," Hathaway said. "Very few petroglyphs are found on private property, and of those that are, well, the property owners seldom want to part with them. Native American heritage and such. My supplier, however, is happy to sell me his endless stock of petroglyphs. I'm told they cover an entire canyon wall."

"How do we know it's real?" Pablo said.

Keep him talking, Pablo thought. *About anything. He mentioned a canyon wall. He's getting careless. Maybe he'll slip up again.*

Hathaway said, "I can assure you this is no forgery, uh…"

"The name's Pablo."

"Yes, Pablo. Very…Missouri did you say?"

"Yes, Missouri."

"All our rock art comes with a Document of Authen-

ticity, which is signed by one of the most respected archaeologists in the Southwest. Dr. Spencer Duke from the
University of New Mexico in Albuquerque."

"Really?" Kiki said, pretending to be impressed.

"Yes, really. Dr. Duke carbon dates the rock varnish on
all of our pieces," Hathaway said. "Rocks exposed to harsh
conditions in arid landscapes often develop a reddish-brown
coating called varnish. It is really nothing more than bacteria,
and these microscopic bacteria can be carbon dated. Are you
familiar with carbon dating?"

"Yes," Kiki said. "I've read about it."

"Oh, sure, I know all about it," Pablo fibbed.

"What is it?" Pia said.

"I'll explain it later," Kiki said.

"The fact is, children, all of our petroglyphs are carbon
dated."

"So if we were to buy Death of a Bison," Kiki said in a
very grown-up voice, "I assume you could produce a bill of
sale from the land owner?"

Truman Hathaway looked at Kiki, but said nothing. He
appeared stunned by the question.

Kiki tried on a pretend smile. It fit perfectly. "Did you
understand my question?"

A vein in Hathaway's forehead swelled. It was the only
indication that he was upset, and in calm voice, he said, "Now
you listen to me, each of you…" He glared at each of them.

"My petroglyphs have been acquired legally and I have worked very hard to make these magnificent rock drawings available to my many customers throughout the world. If you think for one moment that a bunch of rag-tag kids from Missouri are going to come into my store and—"

"You stole those petroglyphs from my Uncle Antonio," Pia cried, gesturing at the petroglyphs in the glass counter. "You cut them out of the boulders in Petroglyph Canyon!"

The cat's out of the bag, Pablo thought. *It's time to get serious.*

Truman Hathaway's eyes glowed red with rage.

"If you don't have a bill of sale from the land owner," Pablo said, "then your petroglyphs must have been stolen." Pablo's legs were trembling. He had never confronted an adult with so much vigor.

"That's right," Kiki said, "show us a bill of sale and we'll be on our way."

Hathaway was speechless.

"And I think the police would love to know more about all this," Kiki said, producing her phone. The I'm-going-to-call-the-police routine had worked with Ginger Gideon. Maybe it would work with Truman Hathaway. "I can see the newspaper headline now: Santa Fe Art Dealer Arrested in Theft of Prehistoric Petroglyphs."

That brought a laugh from Hathaway. "Yes, please do, call the police. The Santa Fe Chief of Police is a man named

Cesar Montano. I'll even give you his private number. Tell him all about your theory. Tell him all about these so-called stolen glyphs that are being sold in my store. Then also tell him how much I enjoyed dinner with him and his wife last Saturday night at the Inn of the Governors." Bent slightly at the waist, Hathaway clapped his hands and laughed again.

Susan DeCell had been in the shipping and receiving room taking inventory. When she heard the ruckus she came out onto the floor and hurried over to where her boss stood arguing with his three young customers.

"Can I help, Mr. Hathaway?"

Hathaway shook his head and dismissed her with a wave of his hand.

"We're just trying to determine who has been stealing our uncle's petroglyphs," Pablo said. "We found a partial glyph at the site and it matched up perfectly with another partial glyph you sold to the Running Tree Art Gallery. We understand you sell partial glyphs—" Pablo ended the thought abruptly. He silently scolded himself. He had promised Ginger Gideon that he would not disclose that information.

Sorry, Ginger, he said to himself.

Hathaway threw back his head and laughed again. "Yes, I know the owner of the Running Tree. Her name is Ginger Gideon. She's a pathological liar. Did you ever stop to think that she was the one looting your uncle's petroglyphs?" He paused, looked at each of them, and said, "Well?"

"No," Pablo said. "That really hadn't occurred to us."

"If your uncle is so interested in preserving his precious rock drawings," Hathaway said, "he should document them. I assume he hasn't, am I right?"

Pablo nodded. He remembered his uncle's words about not having the time to document his beautiful glyphs. "No, he hasn't."

"He should have photographs taken of each glyph and a detailed drawing made of the Mother Rock. The Mother Rock is the rock that is home to the glyph. Then he should take GPS readings to establish the exact location of each Mother Rock. No thief in his right mind would steal glyphs that have been documented. Am I going too fast for you?"

"No," Kiki snarled, "you're not going too fast for us."

There was another long, awkward pause.

"If you must know," Hathaway said, "I get my glyphs from a rancher in Utah. There are hundreds of rock drawings on canyon walls at his ranch." He looked at each of them. "Now, are you satisfied?"

"I suppose so," Pablo said, still unconvinced.

"Now it's time for you children to make your exit," Hathaway said, making a sweeping gesture toward the door. "If not, then I'll be the one calling Police Chief Montano, and I know from experience that he doesn't take kindly to shoplifters." An evil smile stretched Hathaway's scrawny lips. He looked at Pia, his eyes dancing with mischief. "And

I'm certain I saw the brat here sticking a turquoise ring in her pants pocket."

"I'm no brat, and if you steal any more of my uncle's petroglyphs, we're going to be waiting for you and take your picture," Pia said in a shrill voice, one that was about an octave higher than usual.

"Then maybe I should come at night," Hathaway laughed. He straightened his leather jacket with an I-think-we're-done-here tug and walked away.

What did he mean by that? Pablo thought

Chapter 10

"What do you think, Pablo?" Kiki asked.

They were seated on a bench in the Santa Fe Plaza, across the street from the National Bank of Santa Fe. Uncle Antonio had called ten minutes earlier from the bank. His business was almost done, and he would meet them in the plaza.

"I think Truman Hathaway is stealing Uncle Antonio's petroglyphs," Pablo said. "If he came by them legally he wouldn't have made such a big deal over the bill of sale. That was smart of you, Kiki, to ask him about a bill of sale."

"Business people get bills of sale for everything," Kiki explained. "They need some sort of paperwork when they do their taxes. Dad taught me that." Kiki's father ran an advertising agency in Kansas City.

"Now I see the point in documenting petroglyphs," Pablo said.

"Why?" Pia asked.

"If Uncle Antonio had photographs of all his rock

106

drawings, we could compare the photos to the glyphs Hathaway is selling."

"Exactly," Kiki said. "That would prove he had broken the law."

"Hathaway's Death of a Bison is a good example," Pablo said. "If we had a photo of that glyph in the Mother Rock, we'd have proof that it was stolen. I know it's the same rock drawing that Uncle Antonio told us about."

Kiki nodded in agreement.

Pablo glared at his sister. "Way to go, Pia. You told Hathaway if he tried to steal another glyph we were going to take his picture. That's the last secret I'll ever tell you."

"Sorry," Pia said quietly.

"Hathaway's too arrogant for his own good," Kiki said.

Pablo looked at his sister. Before she could ask, he said, "Arrogant means he's too big for his britches."

"We need to document the remaining glyphs before any more are stolen," Kiki said, her voice filled with conviction.

"Ditto that," Pablo said.

"You mean photograph them?" Pia asked.

Pablo nodded. "Photograph them. Sketch the Mother Rocks. Take GPS readings."

"That's a lot of work, Pablo," Kiki said. "We only have three more days at the ranch."

"I think we can do it in three days," Pablo said confidently.

A bearded man with a NY Yankees ball cap came over to them and asked if could sketch each of them. Only ten dollars for all three. He carried an easel, a stool, and some pencils.

Pablo told him no thanks. The man mumbled something under this breath and walked away.

"Kiki, did you see all those patches Hathaway had on his leather jacket?" Pablo asked.

"There was a bunch. I didn't read them all."

"Well, I did, and one read: New Mexico Helicopter Association. Does that ring any bells? Helicopter?"

"Hmmm, I wonder…" Kiki said, deep in thought. She flipped open her phone and accessed the Internet.

"What are you looking for?" Pia asked, craning her neck to see the tiny phone screen.

"If Hathaway does own a helicopter that will be easy enough to prove," Kiki said cunningly.

She keyed in the search words: Santa Fe Municipal Airport. In a second or two, she said, "Here's the telephone number for the Santa Fe airport." She quickly dialed the number, waited a few seconds, and then said, "Yes, this is Susan DeCell. I work for Truman Hathaway and I was wondering if his helicopter has been serviced this week?" Kiki waited for another few seconds, smiled broadly, and then said, "Oh, well, maybe I misunderstood him. I'll ask him if *nice sense for detail, well told in dialog.*

he's wants it serviced again." Pause. "Okay, thanks." She hung up.

"Who is Susan DeCell?" Pia asked.

"The clerk at Hathaway's store," Kiki said. "I read her nametag."

"So...does he have a helicopter?" Pablo said.

"He has a helicopter," Kiki replied, a wide grin pulling at her lips. She typed in new search words. "This is starting to get interesting."

"What are you looking for now?" Pablo said, leaning in as best he could to snatch a glimpse of the miniature screen.

"Santa Fe government." Kiki's finger moved over the screen purposefully.

"I don't get it," Pablo said.

"It may be a long shot, but I want to know more about Hathaway's Fine Art Gallery." Kiki paused while some data downloaded. "I'm going to see if Santa Fe has its business licenses online. Every retail business has to have a license issued by the city." She paused and grinned. "Yep, here they are, hundreds of them. They're listed alphabetically." She peered intensely at the computer screen. "Now, let's find Hathaway's Fine Art Galley." In a few seconds her grin widened into a broad smile. "Here it is!"

"What does it say?" Pia asked.

Kiki enlarged the data on the screen and began to read it: "Hathaway's Fine Art Gallery is one of Santa Fe's most prestigious art galleries. It is located at 4044 Canyon Road in Santa Fe. It specializes in original Southwest artworks, Native American jewelry, blah, blah, blah."

Kiki's eyes suddenly widened. "This is too cool!"

"What?" Pablo said, trying to glimpse the screen.

"The business was established in 2008 by, and I'm quoting: Harvey Ragland D.B.A. Truman Hathaway."

"What's D.B.A.?" Pablo said.

"Doing Business As. It's a business term," Kiki said. "It means that Harvey Ragland is Doing Business As Hathaway's Fine Art Gallery!" Kiki looked at Pablo and Pia with an excited spark in her voice. "Don't you see? He changed his name for the business. He's one of the Ragland brothers. There are four brothers, not three!"

"Are you sure?" Pablo said.

"It's too much of a coincidence. How many people with the name Ragland can there be? I'll bet he and his brothers are the ones stealing the petroglyphs, Pablo," Kiki insisted. "He flies to Petroglyph Canyon in his helicopter with one or more of his brothers, and the brothers do the dirty work of removing the glyphs."

"That seems too simple," Pablo said.

"How else could they steal the glyphs? If they made the trip by car or even horseback to Petroglyph Canyon they would be on Bar-7 land and Uncle Antonio would be sure to see them," Kiki persisted. "Uncle Antonio said so himself."

"Kiki's right, Pablo," Pia said. "Uncle Antonio would see them."

But Pablo wasn't convinced. "We need to do more research. We also need to know how they cut them out of the Mother Rock."

***

It was a quiet ride from Santa Fe back to the Bar-7. Uncle Antonio didn't say ten words, and Pablo could tell from the worn expression on his uncle's face that his meeting at the Santa Fe bank had not gone well.

Pia and Kiki had fallen asleep in the back seat, and Pablo was left alone with his own thoughts. He had finally arrived at the same conclusion Kiki had come to. She was right. It was too much of a coincidence that the owner of the Santa Fe gallery who was selling petroglyphs had the same last name as a trio of cattle-butchering hoodlums who lived within an hour's ride by horseback from Petroglyph Canyon. And Hathaway's Death of a Bison glyph was Uncle Antonio's Barbed Buffalo.

Pablo recounted the story about finding the Barbed Buffalo at Truman Hathaway's store, but Uncle Antonio seemed lost in his own thoughts. Even when Pablo told him that Truman Hathaway's real name was Harvey Ragland, Uncle Antonio seemed not to be listening.

Pablo cleared his mind and rolled his new and revised

plan over and over in his mind. (He wasn't sharing his plan with anyone this time.) He couldn't shake Truman Hathaway's parting comment from his mind: "Then maybe I should come at night." The tone he had used was too convincing. Daylight raids were becoming too risky for him now that he knew three kids were on the case, and future looting would probably occur at night.

It made perfect sense.

They had just turned off New Mexico State Highway 285 and onto Interstate-40 heading east toward the Bar-7 when Uncle Antonio mumbled gravely under his breath: "One hundred and nineteen days without rain. Worst drought ever."

Chapter 11

"Pablo, how does this look?" Pia held up her yellow pad for her brother to admire.

"Another good one, Pia," Pablo said, studying it closely. "Nice job!"

Pia's eyes lit up and she flashed a big smile. "Thanks, Pablo."

Pia had drawn the sandstone Mother Rock and the six individual petroglyphs that resided there: a small herd of elk, a coyote-like animal, two large triangles, a pinwheel-like symbol, four wavy lines, and a circle with a three dots in its center. She had also written down the size of each. Aunt Helen had provided a tape measure.

Kiki stepped over to where Pia sat perched on the edge of a boulder, and peeked over her shoulder. "Perfect, cuz!" Kiki gushed. "Nice job on the elks!"

Pia looked up at Kiki and grinned. "This is fun."

They had arrived at Petroglyph Canyon a little after

dawn and tied their horses in the shade of *Arbol Grande* near the mouth of the canyon.

The information Kiki accessed from the Internet about documenting petroglyphs was very direct: Recording is a three-step procedure: One – measure and draw each rock art symbol; Two – photograph it; Three – map it with a Global Positioning System. The most efficient recording involves a three-person team of artist-measurer, photographer, and mapper.

They had started the long process of documenting the canyon's ancient rock drawings in the early morning coolness, each of them with a separate task.

Pablo photographed each glyph with his camera-phone from different angles, and Kiki took a GPS reading with her phone. Pablo noted the GPS readings at the bottom of each page. Most of the rock drawings were elementary and simple for Pia to draw. Others, however, required a little more finesse.

It was now one hundred and twenty days since it had rained.

The amateur archaeologists had started near the mouth of the wilderness gorge, and began working their way north toward the end of the canyon nearly a mile away. It was a long, tedious process, and by noon they had covered little more than a few hundred feet.

For most of the morning they had worked in the shade,

but now the sun was directly above them, baking the canyon and everything in it. They took frequent water breaks in the patches of shade provided by the huge Mother Rocks.

"This is harder than I thought," Pablo said, examining the photos he had captured.

"How many petroglyphs do you think there are?" Pia asked.

"A lot," Pablo said. He took a big gulp of water from his canteen.

"I'd guess several hundred," Kiki said. "Maybe as many as a thousand."

Kiki had done some research on her phone after arriving back at the ranch from their Santa Fe trip. She had gone to the Internet and discovered that all documentation of New Mexico petroglyphs should be submitted to the Archaeological Society of New Mexico, located at the state capital in Santa Fe. The Society, in turn, would submit the documents to the archaeological archives for the State of New Mexico.

"It'll be worth it, though, huh, Pablo?" Pia said. She was sitting in the shade fanning herself with her hat.

"Yep. Nobody in his right mind would think to steal—"

"Dago Te!"

They whirled around to see Charlie Pecos standing not ten feet away.

Kiki uttered a soft, startled moan, and Pia immediately

placed her hand over her heart, her breath coming in short, audible spurts.

"Charlie Pecos!" Pablo said in a loud, surprised voice. "Where the heck did you come from?"

"I can feel my heart beating, Pablo," Pia said, her eyes as big as egg yolks.

"Charlie Pecos," Kiki began, almost choking on her own words. "I wish you would please announce yourself. You scared the you-know-what out of us again."

"Dago Te!" Charlie Pecos repeated, holding up his hand as a sign of greeting.

"Dago Te!" the three of them said in unison, raising their hands.

"I see that you are saving the stories of my ancestors," Charlie said, glancing at Pia's drawings.

Sampson the Wonder Dog stood nearby wagging his tail, his tongue hanging out the side of his mouth.

"We're documenting them, Charlie," Pablo said.

"Then nobody will steal them," Pia said.

"We hope nobody will steal them," Kiki added.

"What you do is a good thing," Charlie said, eyeing Pia's drawings again. "My ancestors would be proud."

"Where's Moses?" Pia asked, looking about.

Charlie said he had hobbled Moses, and then tied him to *Arbol Grande*.

Charlie came over to where Kiki was standing. He seemed interested in her phone.

"It's a cell phone, Charlie. A cell phone with all kinds of features, including a GPS." She cued the GPS icon, and Charlie studied the image on the screen. "It can also take me to the Internet." Kiki pushed the Internet icon and the Google home page appeared. "I can find the answer to just about any question in the world on the Internet."

"This Internet," Charlie said, "where is it?"

Kiki laughed softly. "Well, uh, I'm not certain, Charlie." She looked at Pablo. "Where's the Internet, cuz?"

"Hmmm, well, let's see…" Pablo said, deep in thought. "To tell you the truth, I'm not sure." He looked at Pia. "Where's the Internet, Pia?"

"That's a silly question," Pablo's sister said. "Everybody knows where the Internet is. It's in all those wires and stuff that's in the back of the computer."

Pablo looked at Kiki with a shrug and a grin, as if you say: "That's as good an explanation as any."

Charlie said, "And you can find the answer to many questions on this Internet?"

"Yes, Charlie, you can," Kiki replied.

Charlie Pecos smiled. "Can you find the answer to that?" He pointed at a series of wavy lines on the nearby Mother Rock. A set of five three-foot-long wavy lines stretched across the base of the boulder. The lines ran horizontal with the ground and were each separated by no more than three inches. It was one of the larger glyphs.

"You got me, Charlie," Kiki said with a small laugh. "No, I can't find an answer to the meaning of that glyph on the Internet, although there are dozens of Internet sites about Southwest rock art." She smiled coyly at the old Apache man. "Can you tell us the meaning?"

"There is an old Indian saying: 'When the wisdom-keepers speak, all should listen.'"

"But it's not that easy to hear their voices, Charlie," Pablo said. "These glyphs are difficult to understand."

"Tell us the meaning of these wavy lines," Kiki said eagerly.

The old man nodded. "The tribe that once lived in this canyon is giving thanks to their river," Charlie said, stepping closer to the Mother Rock, his eyes fixed on the sandstone drawing.

"What river, Charlie?" Pia said. "There aren't any rivers. It's just dust and cactus and lizards. The closest river is, gosh, I'm not sure."

"The closest river," Pablo said, "is the Rio Grande, which runs through Albuquerque, and it's more than sixty miles away."

"That is true," Charlie said, his expression suddenly animated, his eyes alive with energy. "But many years ago, many thousands of years in the past, Dry Creek was once a healthy river. It was filled with live water."

"Live water?" Pablo said. He had heard the term, but couldn't remember its meaning.

"It is water that lives each day. It is always there. It does not come only with the rain or sit idle like a pond." He ran his callused fingers gently over the series of wavy lines. "They are giving thanks to their river. It is their river of life. It nourishes them. It gives them strength. It makes their corn grow. It provides drinking water for their tribe and for their animals. The river is their reason for being."

"It's hard to imagine Dry Creek having live water," Pablo said.

"Even today, if you follow Dry Creek into the Burro Mountains, the water becomes live," Charlie said. "Sadly, it cannot make the journey across the plains. It cannot make the journey to the Bar-7."

"It's been a hundred and twenty days since it rained, Charlie," Pia said, a note of sadness in her voice.

"Yes, child, I know. All the animals suffer."

Pablo tried to visualize Dry Creek flowing down from the Burro Mountains. It was probably no more than a trickle of water at first, but if a person climbed higher the creek probably grew deeper and wider.

Charlie Pecos passed his hand over the surrounding landscape. "Before the walls of this canyon began to fall, this place was once filled with a lush pasture. Both sides of Dry Creek, for as far as the eye could see, overflowed with oceans of long-stemmed grass. The prairies on the land above the canyon were home to buffalo and elk and large herds of deer. New Mexico was once green and full of many living things. Live water made it so."

"What about this glyph, Charlie?" Kiki asked, pointing to two triangles, the first with sides about ten inches long, and the second with sides about half that. "We can't decide what it means."

"I'll bet you understand it, don't you, Charlie?" Pia beamed.

Charlie nodded his head deliberately. "In those ancient times, many families traveled from place to place with no real home. They were called the Voyagers. They were the travelers of Mother Earth. They lived from day to day with no real purpose. They lived on the scraps of food they found in their travels, often eating the remains of dead animals they found during their journey."

Charlie touched the larger triangle. "The large figure is of the village that once called this canyon home. It is the symbol for a large teepee. It is the symbol for a village. The smaller teepee is that of a family of Voyagers. The Voyagers have found a home. They have joined the village. This is the story of that union."

Pablo paused to consider all that Charlie Pecos had told

them, and for one brief moment—his imagination at work—he saw the canyon as it might have looked thousands of years earlier, full of people working, children playing, and animals grazing. Teepees and huts like the one lived in by Charlie Pecos on Saddle Horn Mesa dotted the canyon floor, which was thick with foliage.

"But now we must move to the present," Charlie said, a sudden seriousness in his tone. There is another old Indian saying: 'Don't let yesterday use up too much of today.'"

"What do you mean, Charlie?" Pia said.

"I mean we must concentrate our thoughts on the things that matter at this very moment. I mean you are being watched, children." He raised his eyes to the rim of the canyon.

"By who?" Pablo asked, looking up at the canyon rim. "The Ragland brothers?"

"Yes," Charlie said. "They hover over this canyon like a mother hen hovering over her chicks. They do not like what you are doing. They feel threatened by your efforts to save the rock drawings." The Mescalero Apache continued to gaze at the canyon rim. "The man they call Pirate has been perched up there most of the day watching you. He drove his old truck here early this morning. Most of his time is spent drawing pictures. But he also watches each of you from time to time."

"We saw him the first day we visited this canyon," Pablo said.

"Pirate is their lookout man these days," Charlie said. "Several months ago, all three came many times to this canyon to examine the rock drawings, and later the helicopter came, and later still the helicopter came and the rock drawings began to disappear."

"The Ragland brothers must have told Hathaway about the glyphs," Kiki surmised. "How else would he have known?"

"Exactly," Pablo said.

"They won't hurt us, will they, Charlie?" Pia said, her eyes fixed on the ragged canyon rim one hundred feet above.

"Not as long as Charlie Pecos is near," Charlie said.

Chapter 12

It was late that afternoon when Pirate arrived back at Axe Handle after a day of spying on Pablo, Pia, and Kiki. He parked the old Chevy pickup in front of the Silver Nugget Hotel and went inside. He found his brothers in the lobby of the run-down hotel. They were killing time, an activity at which they were abundantly experienced.

The Ragland brothers lived ("survived" would be a better word) in what had once been the most elegant hotel in Axe Handle, New Mexico. These days, the hotel's roof leaked, the walls were drafty, and the place had no plumbing—there was an outhouse out back—but it was home to the three brothers. They enjoyed living at the hotel for two reasons: There were no noisy neighbors to monitor their criminal activities, and the rent was free.

Axe Handle had once been a very prosperous silver mining town. Indeed, in 1910 it claimed more than two thousand inhabitants. But by 1940 the rich veins of Burro Mountain silver had played out. The Silver Nugget Hotel closed its doors in 1958, and now the town's only residents consisted of the Ragland brothers, a few prairie dogs, a coyote or two, and several families of rattlesnakes.

A couple of times each month one of the brothers would drive their 1965 Chevy pickup into Sierra Vista and barter slabs of Bar-7 beef for the provisions they needed. When barter didn't work they would resort to stealing. If the brothers were really down on their luck, which was just about always, they would send Pirate into Sierra Vistas to wait in line for food stamps at the New Mexico State Social Services office.

Red and Gordo looked up as their one-eyed brother pushed through the door and entered the hotel lobby. Red was practicing his knife-throwing skills. His favorite target was a bull's eye he'd drawn on the wall. Gordo was seated in a plastic patio chair reading a *Superman* comic book.

Red's cellphone, the one given to him by Truman Hathaway, D.B.A. Harvey Ragland, was gathering dust on an empty orange crate. For most of the afternoon Red had been watching the phone like a hungry hawk perched in a tree watching a field mouse. Throw the knife, stare at the phone; throw the knife, stare at the phone. But the phone had been silent all day.

Pirate went over to where several tin cups were hanging on the wall. He dipped his cup into a nearby water barrel. The water was warm and had a strange mineral taste, (it also had a horrible smell) but it was wet, and Pirate was thirsty. He drank the cup empty.

"Truck's been acting up again," Pirate reported, looking over at Red. "Carburetor's bad. Cutting out something awful. Just about didn't make it back from the canyon."

"Don't be telling me about no carburetor," Red snarled. "Tell me about them kids. Was they there…there in the canyon?" He hurled his knife across the room. It stuck inches away from the bull's eye, which was littered with hundreds of knife points. "Or was ya too busy drawing pictures to notice?"

"I didn't sketch none today," Pirate said, insulted.

"I know what ya do when ain't nobody around," Red growled. "So was they there?"

"Yeah, they was there. They was taking pictures and stuff," Pirate replied. "That Apache fellow was there, too."

"That Injun is sticking his nose into our business," Gordo protested, looking up from his comic book. "Them kids is taking pictures of them glyphs and Charlie Pecos is right there like maybe he's some sort of protector or something."

"So you just up and left?" Red said, glaring at Pirate. He walked across the room and pulled his knife out of the wall, and then gazed for a few brief moments at the phone, as if staring at it would make it ring.

"What the heck could I do, Red? That Apache fellow

might be old and all, but I've done seen him ride and rope. He ain't nearly as old as a body might think," Pirate said. "Besides, he's got some sort of crazy throwing stick he uses."

"Throwing stick?" Red asked, standing motionless and staring at his one-eyed brother.

"Yeah, throwing stick."

"We got guns, he's got himself a stick, and you're whimpering?" A menacing gleam flashed in Red's eyes. "I'm glad our pappy ain't alive to see you, Albert Ragland. He'd be right disappointed."

Red walked back to his throwing spot.

"I've seen him use that curved stick," Pirate said. "He can knock a quail out of the sky with it."

"You're a numskull!" Red barked, drawing back his arm and hurling his knife with all his might. The blade swished through the air and struck the wall with a deadly *Thud*! a few inches from the bull's eye. He turned back toward Pirate. "So ya just watched and did nothing?"

"Maybe I shoulda dropped a rock on them?" Pirate complained. "Is that what I shoulda done?"

Red mumbled something under his breath, and then spit a wad of chewing tobacco onto the rotting hotel floor. He glanced at the phone again.

"I'm telling ya, Red, them kids is putting us out of business," Gordo said, making his case a second time. "Bad timing for the Ragland boys. Yes, sir, bad timing."

"Shut your trap!" Red roared.

Pirate went over and slumped into an old recliner the brothers had salvaged from the Sierra Vista city dump. "I watched them kids for most of the day," Pirate said. "The three of them was taking pictures and making sketches."

"Hathaway said we ain't gonna steal them glyphs that's been photographed," Red reported. "Too risky."

"So how will we know which glyphs to cut and which glyphs not to cut?" Gordo said.

"You let me worry about that," his redheaded brother said.

"It ain't fair," Gordo said in a quiet voice.

"What ain't fair?" Red said, glaring defiantly at his plus-size brother.

"We do all the work and Hathaway gets them glyphs," Gordo said. "It ain't fair."

Gordo struggled to his feet, and then hauled his enormous carcass over to what was once the hotel's check-in desk. He popped open a large plastic container that was sitting there. The container was filled with flour tortillas—they were as brittle as sandpaper—and Gordo wrapped his plump fingers around one.

Red looked at his obese brother. "How much cash you got in your wallet?"

"Huh?"

"Money. How much ya got?"

"Don't know. Maybe ten dollars." He broke the rock-hard flour tortilla apart and stuffed one-half of it into his mouth.

"And how much would you have if Hathaway wasn't cutting us in?"

"That don't make no—"

"How much?" Red Ragland pressed.

Gordo paused, and then said, "None."

"Then quit your whining," Red said. "It ain't much now, but things will get better after we cut us a few more of them glyphs."

At that moment, Red's cell phone rang. Finally. The tobacco-chewing cowboy hurried over and snatched the phone off the orange crate. His lips moving over each word, he read the text message. With an open-mouthed stare, he read the message again.

"Hathaway done texted me," Red told his brothers. "He's got us a plan to keep those nosey kids outta the canyon."

"So what's the plan?" Gordo asked, stuffing the other half of the tortilla into his mouth.

Red looked across the room at Pirate, his mouth drawn back into a frozen grin. "How long to fix that carburetor?"

***

Hunger had forced the pregnant Diamondback rattler to leave her den that night. She had not eaten in nearly a month. Two hours after leaving her Dry Creek hole the female pit viper cornered a Kangaroo Rat in its own den, and then killed and ate it. The infrared detectors called "pits" allowed the snake to locate her warm-blooded prey in total darkness.

Her hunt, however, had taken the poisonous reptile far from her den, and now she sought warmth because she could feel her babies stirring inside her. She needed a cozy little place to deliver. Flicking her forked tongue and tasting the air, the snake crawled up to the wooden building, found a loose slat, and then climbed under it and slithered inside.

The five-foot rattler immediately sensed the vibrations of people talking.

***

"Nite, Pablo!" Pia said, slipping into the bottom bunk and pulling the covers up around her neck.

"Nite, Pia!" Pablo said, standing in the doorway. "Nite, Kiki!"

Kiki crawled up onto the top bunk, fluffed her pillow, and wiggled under the covers. "Good night, Pablo Perez!" she sang. "Sleep tight and don't let the bedbugs bite!"

"Not a chance," Pablo chimed.

"Are we going to document some more glyphs tomorrow?" Pia said.

"You bet," Pablo said.

"How fun!" Pia squealed.

"See you for breakfast, Pablo," Kiki said.

"Ditto that," Pablo replied.

Pablo walked across the shadowy bunkhouse hallway and into his room. He switched off the light, and then stretched out on the bottom bunk fully clothed. The glitter of a full moon shone into his room through a small window.

"A full moon—perfect," he said softly.

Somewhere in the darkness outside a hoot owl announced its presence with a *Who! Who!*

Pablo lay in bed quietly thinking about the needless destruction of Petroglyph Canyon and its timeless rock drawings. The looting had to stop, and he wrapped his mind around his plan to catch the Ragland brothers in the act of stealing a glyph. It was a simple plan.

Simple plans seem to work best, he thought. The simpler the plan, the better.

He had not shared his daring scheme with Pia or Kiki. Had he told them, they would have insisted on joining him, and Pablo wanted to avoid that because there was some danger in the plan, even though it was only a five or less on the Danger Scale of ten. Concealment was also key to his plan, and one person could remain concealed far better than three.

Pablo lay quietly on his bunk for fifteen minutes, and

then got up and slipped into his jacket. He stuffed his camera phone into one jacket pocket and a small flashlight into the other.

He tiptoed across the hallway. Pablo detected movement of some sort on the hallway floor, but dismissed it as full-moon shadows. He paused at Pia and Kiki's open door and listened. He could hear their heavy breathing, and he was certain they were fast asleep.

Pablo slipped out the back door of the bunkhouse and hurried across the barnyard toward the stables, Charlie Pecos' remark earlier that day rummaging through Pablo's brain: "… you are being watched, children."

If Charlie was right—and Pablo was a hundred percent sure that he was—then there was good reason to think the Ragland brothers would not attempt to continue looting the canyon during the day. There were simply too many witnesses. The Raglands' future raids would be conducted at night, and Pablo was determined to be one step ahead of them. He would be waiting when they arrived, camera-phone in hand.

Chapter 13

The full moon silhouetted the ranch house and the many corrals and outbuildings, and once Pablo's eyes adjusted to the flat, vague light, navigating across the barnyard was easy.

There were no lights in the main ranch house. Uncle Antonio and Aunt Helen had likewise turned in for the night, and Pablo continued across the barnyard toward the stable. He hurried through the open stable door and went directly to Buster's stall. The big stallion grunted a welcome in the spotty darkness as Pablo entered the stall. Pablo flipped the light switch, and the cubicle was bathed in a soft, clean light.

"You ready to do some work tonight, big fellow?" Pablo asked in a quiet voice, rubbing Buster's neck. The brown and white Paint pawed at the sawdust and raised his ears, almost as if he understood Pablo's words.

"It's just you and me against the Ragland brothers, Buster. It could be a little dangerous. Are you up for a little danger?"

The big Paint uttered a soft whinny.

"Good, that makes two of us," Pablo said. "The Ragland brothers have stolen their last glyph from Uncle Antonio and Aunt Helen."

Five minutes later, Buster was saddled and ready to go. Pablo took the reins, flipped off the light, and then led Buster out of the stable, around the adjacent empty hay barn, and down a slight incline to Dry Creek. When he reached the creek's sandy floor, Pablo swung up into the saddle—he gave Buster a soft kick in the ribs. The big stallion began trotting down the dry riverbed bed toward Petroglyph Canyon. The full moon hung in the sky like a big pearl. It was so bright that horse and rider cast a shadow in the dusty wash.

Pablo touched the camera phone in his jacket pocket to make sure it was still there. The camera phone was key to his plan. If a picture was worth a thousand words, then a picture of the Ragland brothers cutting a petroglyph from the Mother Rock with their rock saw should be worth ten times that. In fact, it should be worth enough to put them in prison for a couple of years. But more importantly, it would end the senseless destruction of the ancient rock drawings.

Pablo was certain the Ragland brothers would change their method of attack from day to night. He was also certain they needed bright lights. Surely they weren't stupid enough to use a rock saw in the dark of night with only flashlights. They would bring portable lights to work by, which would generate enough illumination for his camera phone to capture the criminal images.

Pablo felt connected somehow to the glyphs. He wasn't sure why.

***

Trotting at a leisurely pace, Buster made the trip to the mouth of Petroglyph Canyon in less than an hour. Pablo reined in the big stallion, and scanned the terrain surrounding *Arbol Grande*.

"No helicopter, Buster. We're here first."

Pablo tied Buster to a piñon tree a short distance from the mouth of the canyon. If the Ragland brothers traveled by helicopter to the canyon, and if they landed their helicopter at the usual spot near *Arbol Grande*, Buster would be far enough away that he would not be seen.

Pablo wasn't entirely certain the Raglands would come by helicopter. Night flying might prove too dangerous. If they didn't come by helicopter, he was sure they would drive down Dry Creek to the canyon. One way or another, the Raglands would appear—Pablo was sure of it.

"Try and keep a low profile, Buster," Pablo said, stroking the horse's neck. "And if you hear a helicopter or a pickup, chill out. The Ragland brothers want the petroglyphs, not you."

Buster pawed at the sand and seemed to nod his head.

Pablo walked back to the mouth of the canyon and stared into it. The canyon always looked forbidding, even during the daylight, but under a full moon it looked, well, downright scary. Pablo could feel a trickle of fear race through his body. But, as it had happened before, Pablo somehow felt energized by it. Fear somehow gave him courage. Without fear there would be no courage, and he set off, his stride energetic, following the beam from his flashlight into the mysterious canyon.

He paused a few yards inside the narrow mouth of the wilderness gorge. The ghostly canyon shadows seemed to flutter in the cool night air. They almost seemed alive.

He listened for the nauseous sound of a rock saw or the unmistakable vibration of helicopter blades beating against the nighttime sky, but all he heard was a June wind moaning softly along the steep walls of the wilderness gorge.

Then, somewhere in the darkness, a *Yip-Yip-Yip* stirred the air. In a few moments, a second *Yip-Yip-Yip* replied.

Coyotes, Pablo thought. *Relax.*

Pablo heard a rustling in the brush off to his right and he turned in that direction. The rustling sound continued for a few more seconds, and then fell silent.

"What was that?" he muttered, his eyes straining in the darkness. He scanned the surrounding rocks and brush with his flashlight. Nothing.

Perhaps it was a jackrabbit snacking on a bush. Or a

Kangaroo Rat heading home with its latest prize. There were also hordes of lizards living in the canyon.

Sure, it was a stupid lizard, he told himself. *Relax.*

Petroglyph Canyon was also populated with rattlesnakes, and Pablo sensed his beating heart. He could hear it in his ears.

He moved deeper into the canyon.

Pablo shone his flashlight beam on the house-sized boulders to get his bearing. Stationing himself in the proper spot was crucial to the success of the mission, and he illuminated the Mother Rock before him. The beam from his flashlight framed an ugly crater in the huge sandstone slab. Beyond the Mother Rock were other huge boulders, their light brown skins tattooed with beautiful, undisturbed rock drawings.

"This is where the Ragland brothers will pick up where they left off," he said softly, the sound of his own voice comforting.

The cone of light moved up the virgin Mother Rock, illuminating each glyph: a beautifully designed half-moon; a face with pointed ears, which resembled a creature out of a horror movie (Pablo wished he hadn't seen that one.); two human footprints, one large, one small; something resembling a fish with two eyes and a mouth; two circles connected by a perpendicular line.

"I couldn't even guess what that's all about," he

muttered, his flashlight beam framing the two-circles-and-a-line glyph. It resembled a barbell.

Pablo stepped back and pointed the beam from his flashlight into a rocky niche at the base of the nearby debris field. He spotted a good hiding place, and he stepped over to the sandstone recess and climbed up into it. He scanned the terrain before him with his flashlight beam. His field of vision covered nearly 180 degrees.

"Perfect," he muttered.

He clicked off his flashlight and checked his cell phone battery. It was full.

He again sensed his beating heart. No, not beating, racing. He tried to swallow, but his throat was as parched as Dry Creek. *Relax*, he told himself. *Okay, try and relax.*

The faraway rumble of thunder echoed softly against the canyon walls, and a dim flash of light washed over the western rim high above.

It's raining somewhere, he thought. But not here. No rain for the Bar-7. One hundred and twenty-one days without rain. Or was it twenty-two? Still the worst drought ever.

Suddenly, some sort of winged creature swooped along the canyon floor before him. The *Flap-Flap-Flap* of wings was followed instantly by the high-pitched squeal of a dying...what?

An owl has caught a rabbit. Or maybe a lizard. Owls

hunt at night. Their eyesight is very good at night. It was an owl, wasn't it?

Relax.

Another dim and distant flash of light slithered over the west canyon rim, followed in a few seconds by a faint rumble of thunder.

It was cold at this altitude, even in the summer, and Pablo rubbed his hands together for warmth. Sleep tugging at him, Pablo closed his eyes for a moment and dozed. In a few short minutes, he was fast asleep.

***

Pia climbed into the top bunk and wormed her body under the covers next to Kiki.

"Are you okay, Pia?" Kiki said quietly, blinking her eyes awake.

"I couldn't sleep. I had a bad dream," Pia said. "I dream-ed a big snake was crawling into our room."

Kiki laughed softly and wrapped an arm around her nine-year-old cousin, drawing her closer. "Do you know the Bad Dream rule?" Kiki asked quietly.

"No."

"If you have a bad dream, wake up, and then go back to sleep, the bad dream is gone."

"Really?"

"Yep."

"Do you really mean that or—" Pia turned her head in the spotty darkness and looked toward the open door. "Did you hear something, Kiki?"

"No, Pia. It's just your imagination. Close your eyes and go back to sleep."

***

Pablo was awakened by the thunderous Apache greeting. It seemed to echo off the canyon walls: *"Dago Te!"*

Pablo jerked awake. He raised his head and opened his eyes. Standing not ten feet away—under the light of a full moon—was an Apache man. His face was painted and he was wrapped in a buffalo robe. He wore a headdress of feathers, and his arms were folded across his chest. Somehow (he wasn't sure how) Pablo knew this man was an Apache chief.

Is this a dream? Pablo wondered.

The Apache chief held up his hand in a sign of greeting. *"Dago Te,* Pablo Perez!"

"Dago Te," Pablo replied hesitantly.

"These stone pictures are the stories of my life and the lives of all who came before me," the man said. "You must fight all those who would destroy them."

"Yes, I will," Pablo said. "I'm waiting for the men who are stealing them. I'm going to take their picture." It suddenly sounded so childish, and for an instant Pablo regretted having devised such a boyish plan.

"You have a warrior's heart, Pablo," the Apache chief said. "There is an old Indian saying: 'One must face fear or forever run from it.' You must once again face fear, Pablo."

"I don't understand, sir."

"The Ragland brothers will not come tonight, and you must return to the ranch at once."

"What?"

"Wake up, Pablo! Pia and Kiki are in danger! There is no time to lose!" And then, in an earsplitting voice, the Apache chief shouted, "WAKE UP, PABLO!"

Pablo awoke with a jerk, this time for real. He looked at his watch: 4:35 a.m. He had been asleep for more than four hours.

Four hours? It seemed like no more than a few short minutes.

The full moon had slipped away, and the canyon was as black as coal.

Pablo realized that he had, indeed, been dreaming. It was a dream, wasn't it? But what had the Apache chief meant? Why did he insist that Pablo return to the ranch? And how did he know the Ragland brothers would not visit the canyon? Why were Pia and Kiki in danger?

Pablo crawled down from his rocky niche, clicked on his flashlight, and ran toward the mouth of the canyon. There was to time to lose.

When he emerged from the mouth of the canyon his cell

phone beeped. He had a text message from Kiki. It read: PABLO HELP!

Chapter 14

Pablo approached the ranch house at a full gallop, the rosy blush of dawn coloring the eastern sky. He and Buster were breathing hard. It had been a fast ten-mile ride, and the big stallion's neck and shoulders were white with sweat. A sick knot had formed in Pablo's stomach, and as the ranch came into view the knot tightened.

There was activity near the rear door of the bunkhouse, and as Pablo rode closer he could make out several figures milling around in the early light of day. A police car was parked at one end of the bunkhouse, the unmistakable shape of beacons silhouetted against the half-light of dawn.

Pablo brought Buster to a sudden stop a few feet from the rear door of the bunkhouse. Swinging down from his saddle, he rushed over to where Uncle Antonio and Aunt Helen stood talking to Sheriff Frost and her deputy, Diego Sanchez. A couple of other men—cowboys that Pablo recognized from the gathering, including the Hispanic cowboy named Billy Soto—were standing off to one side. Pablo could tell by the

142

expressions on everyone's faces that something terrible had happened.

Aunt Helen hurried over and wrapped Pablo in a hug. "Thank heavens, you're...you're okay, Pablo. We thought they had taken you too."

"I'm fine, Aunt Helen," Pablo blurted out. "What happened? What's wrong?"

"They're gone, Pablo!" were the first words out of Uncle Antonio's mouth. "Pia and Kiki have been kidnapped by the Ragland brothers!"

A stinging sense of guilt ripped through Pablo like a white-hot poker.

"Where have you been, Pablo?" Aunt Helen said, stepping back, a flash of impatience in her eyes.

"At the canyon," Pablo replied. "I was going to try and—"

"Doesn't matter where the boy was," Sheriff Maggie Frost said, rolling a toothpick from one side of her mouth to the other. A tall, heavyset woman, Maggie was known for her no-nonsense approach to law and order. "What matters now is that we get the girls back."

The words "get the girls back" filled Pablo with a sense of sadness he had never felt. It was complete and utter sorrow, and for an instant he sensed the burn of tears.

"I should have been here!" Pablo said in a loud voice, angry with himself.

Everyone looked at Pablo, but not a word was spoken, and Pablo said, again in a loud voice, "It's all my fault!"

"That's enough of that kind of talk, Pablo," Uncle Antonio said. "If there's blame to be had, it should be directed at the Ragland brothers. They're the ones to be faulted, Pablo, not you. We'll get the girls back. I know the Ragland boys. They may be thieves, but they're not killers. They won't hurt the girls."

Pablo didn't think Uncle Antonio sounded too convincing.

"Are you sure it was the Raglands?" Pablo said. "Maybe Pia and Kiki rode off in the night looking for me." Pablo looked at all the stern faces. "Did anyone think of that?"

"It was the Raglands, Pablo," Uncle Antonio said in a gloomy, persuasive voice.

Billy Soto came over. He was carrying a five-foot-long rattlesnake by its tail. The pit viper was dead. "Mind if I take the snake, Antonio? Wife makes a mean rattlesnake stew."

"Take it, Billy. Enjoy," Uncle Antonio said, not even hearing his own voice.

"Where'd the snake come from?" Pablo asked, the knot in his stomach sucking the breath out of him.

"Found it on the floor in the girls' room," Sheriff Frost said. "Somebody ran a knife between its eyes. My guess it was Red Ragland. He's pretty handy with a knife."

"I've heard that," Deputy Sanchez said.

"Did it bite anyone?" Pablo asked. "Pia or Kiki…?"

"Hard to say," Billy Soto said. "Might have. Might not have. No way to tell."

Pablo thanked him with a nod, the guilt-ridden thought continuing to torment him: *I should have been here!*

"I'd sure enough stay out of the bunkhouse," Diego Sanchez said. "That dead female rattler gave birth to whole bunch of babies. They're everywhere."

"That's the least of our worries at the moment," Uncle Antonio said soberly.

The big-boned female sheriff looked at Uncle Antonio. Her gaze was intense. "Any idea why the Raglands would kidnap your nieces, Antonio?"

Uncle Antonio nodded sadly. "They meant to put a stop to the kids documenting the glyphs," he replied. "Pure and simple. The Raglands wanted to put a stop to it all."

"I don't get it," Sheriff Frost said. She removed the toothpick from her mouth and dropped it into her shirt pocket.

"The Raglands—leastwise we think it's the Raglands— have been stealing the glyphs, Maggie. Stealing them and selling them." Uncle Antonio recounted the story of Pablo, Pia, and Kiki and the day they visited the Running Tree Art Gallery in Santa Fe.

"I've been to that place," Deputy Sanchez said. "Mostly junk."

"Story on the television news about that place, that

Running Tree Art Gallery," Sheriff Frost said. "Somebody torched the place night before last. Total loss. I wonder if that figures into any of this?"

Pablo recalled Ginger Gideon's description of Truman Hathaway that day in her store. She had used the word "ruthless" to describe Truman Hathaway. Pablo wondered if Hathaway had been the one to torch her store, payback for revealing his name as the supplier of the partial glyphs. He quietly answered his own question. Yes.

"Come to find out," Uncle Antonio continued, "that the owner of another gallery, fellow by the name of Truman Hathaway, was selling glyphs in his store. One of the rock drawings he had for sale showed a buffalo with two spears sticking out of its side."

"And what's so unusual about that, Antonio?" Sheriff Frost said. "Lots of stores in Santa Fe sell glyphs. Most are fakes."

"That may be true, but a rock drawing just like the one at Hathaway's place had been carved out of the Mother Rock a few days earlier in Petroglyph Canyon," Uncle Antonio said. "It was one of my favorites. Even named it: Barbed Buffalo. Kids tell me this Hathaway fellow had renamed it Death of a Bison. Same glyph, Maggie."

A frown crossed Maggie Frost's face.

"And here's the kicker," Uncle Antonio said. "Kids learned Truman Hathaway's real name is Harvey Ragland.

I'm guessing it's Harvey's three brothers that live out there in Axe Handle."

"Those nit-wits still living in that old hotel?" Maggie Frost asked.

"Yep. When they aren't stealing glyphs, they're butchering my cattle."

Pablo had managed to keep silent while Uncle Antonio and Maggie Frost sorted through the facts, but he could contain himself no longer, and the words jumped out of his mouth. "Sheriff, let's drive out to Axe Handle and see if Pia and Kiki are there! We can be there in twenty minutes!"

"I plan to do just that, son," Maggie said, her eyes drawn together thoughtfully. "But you can forget all about 'we.' There is no 'we.' It's just me and my deputy. Savvy?"

"But I think I can—"

"No 'but' about it, son," Maggie ordered. "This kidnapping business could get real—"

Uncle Antonio raised his hand to stop. "No need to go into detail, Maggie."

"Just let us do our job," Maggie Frost told Pablo.

Reluctantly, Pablo nodded.

Maggie turned back toward Uncle Antonio. "That Red Ragland is all the time chewing tobacco, chewing it and spitting the juice, and it doesn't matter whether he's indoors or outdoors. Which leads me to believe it was him since I found some dried tobacco juice on the floor of the girls' room."

The thought of the Ragland brothers dragging Pia and Kiki out of the bunkhouse sent a sharp sliver of anger through Pablo's body.

"But we can't rush these things," Sheriff Frost said. "We need to keep our heads. Need to think this thing out. Personally, I don't think they gave this kidnapping much thought. I'm guessing it was a spur-of-the-moment decision. That Red Ragland has gone off more than once half-cocked."

The lingering image of Red Ragland and his brothers hovering over his sister and cousin continued to fill Pablo's mind with a quiet sort of rage.

Sheriff Frost laughed softly. "There's not one good brain between those three brothers. Stump dumb, all of 'em."

Pablo scowled. It seemed to him that Sheriff Frost was taking the kidnapping much too casually.

"I know all three Ragland brothers," Uncle Antonio said. "Red is mean and Gordo is stupid. Pirate, well, he isn't such a bad sort."

"Are the girls heavy sleepers, Pablo?" Sheriff Frost asked, her expression again grim.

"Don't know about Kiki, but Pia is," Pablo replied. "Sometimes it takes forever to wake her up. She's always late for school."

The drama of the kidnapping unfolded before Pablo in bits and pieces. Aunt Helen said she had been in kitchen searching for her heartburn medicine about three o'clock in the morning when she heard the girls scream from the bunkhouse. Aunt Helen looked at Pablo and said, "I walked to the kitchen door and opened it, then I heard Pia scream your name, Pablo."

The knot in Pablo's stomach tightened again, and the sadness he felt was complete. Guilt tugged at Pablo in one direction, sorrow in the other, and the two threatened to tear him apart. His eyes burning with tears, he turned away to hide his sorrow.

"I hurried and woke Uncle Antonio," Helen Flores said, "and the two of us ran across the barnyard to the bunkhouse—"

"I had my shotgun," Uncle Antonio said.

"—but by the time we arrived, Pia and Kiki were gone." Aunt Helen put her hand to her mouth, smothering a sob.

"We saw taillights in the distance," Uncle Antonio said, gesturing toward the dirt road leading from the ranch house complex and out to New Mexico Highway 59. "Looked like that rattle-trap old Chevy pickup the Raglands drive. Easy to tell in the dark. Those Chevy taillights are a dead giveaway."

"Did you follow them?" Pablo asked, his mind thinking ahead, thinking about how he would find his sister and cousin, thinking about how he would rescue them.

But where do I start? he thought.

Uncle Antonio nodded grimly. "They outsmarted me, Pablo. Removed the battery cables from my truck. By the time I popped the hood and had a look-see, they were long gone."

"Was there a note?" Pablo said, hoping. "Maybe they want something for Pia and Kiki's return."

"No, Pablo," Uncle Antonio said gravely, "there was no note."

Pablo's patience was suddenly at its bitter end. "We're standing around talking when we should be out looking for Pia and Kiki," he said, almost shouting.

"Can't rush these things, son," Maggie Frost repeated. "Need to think this thing through."

Pablo gritted his teeth. "I can't wait to get my hands on Red Ragland," he hissed.

"Now, I don't want to have to tell you again. I don't want you getting in the middle of this thing, son," Sheriff Frost said. "Like I said, it's just me and my deputy. If it is a kidnapping, we'll have to call the federal authorities." The sheriff gave Pablo a hard, stern look. "You let the law take care of this. You just stand back and give us some room to work."

Pablo forced himself to smile and nod.

Not a chance, he thought.

***

At a little before ten that morning, Sheriff Frost and her deputy crept through the back door of the Silver Nugget

Hotel. Sheriff Frost had parked her patrol car some distance away from Axe Handle, and she and Diego Sanchez had hiked in the last mile or so. The 1965 Chevy pickup was parked in back near the barn.

Once inside the old hotel, Sheriff Frost and her deputy paused to listen. The hotel was quiet. The only sound was the creaking of the Silver Nugget Hotel sign, which was hanging from a single nail and swinging in the wind from the second-floor balcony. They tiptoed down the hallway toward the lobby.

Sheriff Frost had been to the old hotel more than once. She had visited the brothers on several occasions in an on-going investigation about the rash of cattle kills at the Bar-7 (among other things), and she knew the brothers lived in the abandoned hotel. Although they each had their own sleeping quarters on the second floor, Maggie knew the trio of misfits spent most of their time in the hotel lobby.

Sheriff Frost and Deputy Sanchez took out their hand-guns as they approached the lobby. They paused once again to listen, but were greeted with silence. Maggie motioned to her deputy that they would enter the lobby on the count of three. Mouthing the words, she held up one finger, two fingers, and then three fingers, and they rushed into the hotel lobby.

"Don't anybody make a move!" Sheriff Frost yelled, waving her revolver in a wide sweeping motion.

"Police! Stay where you are!" Diego Sanchez cried.

But the room was empty.

The Ragland brothers were gone, and there was no sign of Pia or Kiki.

Chapter 15

"Pablo, this is Agent Fred Edwards," Sheriff Frost said. "He's from the FBI's Albuquerque bureau."

Pablo, Uncle Antonio, and Aunt Helen were seated in Sheriff Frost's office in Sierra Vista. Agent Edwards was also seated. Two other FBI agents, both dressed in dark business suits, stood nearby, hands behind their backs. They were both wearing sunglasses, and Pablo thought they looked a little creepy.

Sheriff Frost had called the FBI during the return trip from Axe Handle that morning about ten. The three agents were on the scene by noon.

"This kidnapping has gotten to be more than I can handle," Sheriff Frost said with an uneasy smile, glancing at Antonio and Helen Flores. "It's time for the professionals to step in. Besides, kidnapping is a federal offense."

"Do you have any leads, Mr. Edwards?" Pablo asked, the question flying off his tongue.

"Several," the FBI man said, glancing at the other agents, neither of whom showed the slightest emotion.

Pablo waited for Fred Edwards to speak. When he didn't, Pablo said impatiently, "Would you mind telling us what they are?"

"I'm afraid I can't go into detail, son," the well-groomed FBI agent said. "I simply can't give you any information at this time. I don't want to give anyone…well, false hope, for lack of a better term."

"I need to know about my sister!" Pablo said, the remark delivered in a strong, commanding voice. "And my cousin!"

"I know how you must feel," the FBI man said in a businesslike tone of voice. "But I'm not at liberty to discuss it." He looked at Uncle Antonio. "I want to make sure I understand the reason the girls were kidnapped. You said something earlier about petroglyphs?"

Uncle Antonio turned to Pablo. "Tell him, Pablo."

Pablo nodded. "We were documenting the rock drawings so the Ragland brothers, or anyone else, wouldn't steal them."

The FBI man appeared uncertain. "What would that have—"

"Documented petroglyphs can be traced," Pablo said. "Nobody is going to try and sell a rock drawing that they know has been documented with photographs, sketches, and GPS readings."

"And you think the Raglands were stealing them?"

"We're certain," Pablo said, going into great detail about the day he and his sister and cousin had spent in Santa Fe, and the information Kiki had found on the Internet about Truman Hathaway's real name. He also explained the history of Barbed Buffalo, which Hathaway had renamed Death of a Bison.

"Let me see if I understand this," Agent Fred Edwards said. "The three Ragland brothers are stealing the glyphs and their brother in Santa Fe, a man who goes by the name of Truman Hathaway, is selling them? Is that about right?"

Pablo nodded. "Yes."

Agent Edwards smiled. "You might find this of interest, but this isn't the first time we've had this Hathaway character in our sights."

"He's been arrested before?" Pablo said.

"No, not arrested, just investigated," the FBI man said. "I'll make this as brief as possible." He cleared his throat and began. "Harvey Ragland and his three brothers grew up in Albuquerque. Harvey and the other three men are half-brothers, actually. Same father, different mothers. Harvey, or Truman if you prefer, loves to scam people. It's been a life-long obsession. His specialty is art or art objects. He'd rather sell a counterfeit than an original. Fraud is in his blood, and the works of Georgia O'Keeffe are his house specialty."

"Georgia O'Keeffe," Aunt Helen exclaimed, "I adore her work."

"You'd probably adore the O'Keeffe counterfeits, too. You can't tell the original from the fake," Edwards said. "Hathaway found an artist living in Taos who could turn out a dozen so-called O'Keeffe originals every week. They made a killing. The artist was arrested and did some prison time, but Harvey Ragland claimed he didn't know they were counterfeit, and the artist in Taos wouldn't testify against Ragland because he was afraid of him—the charges against Harvey were dropped. Apparently, Harvey Ragland is one mean customer. Ruthless."

There's that word again, Pablo thought.

"Where'd a low-life like that get the money to open an art gallery in Santa Fe, New Mexico?" Uncle Antonio asked.

Agent Edwards grinned. "Like I said, he made an absolute killing with those O'Keeffe counterfeits. As much as—"

"No offense, Mr. Edwards," Pablo interrupted, "but I need to know about Pia and Kiki. Tell me something. Anything. I need to know."

"Easy, Pablo," Aunt Helen said. "These men are just doing their jobs." She was seated beside Pablo, and she leaned over and gave him a motherly pat him on the knee.

Pablo looked at Aunt Helen, and said, "I'd just like to know Pia and Kiki are okay."

"I know, Pablo," she replied. "We all want the same thing."

Agent Edwards got up and huddled briefly with the two other agents, and then he turned and faced Pablo. "I can tell you this. One of our field agents has spoken by cell phone to a brakeman for the Santa Fe Southern railroad, and the brakeman said he saw several individuals hopping his freight train early this morning. Sometime around ten a.m."

"Where?" Pablo asked.

"Not far from Axe Handle," the FBI man said, glancing at his note pad. "Near the railroad tracks at a place called Suicide Bend."

"But the Ragland brothers own a truck," Pablo said. "Why would they—"

"I'm just telling you what I know," the FBI man said. And then, looking at Uncle Antonio, he said, "Are you familiar with this place called Suicide Bend?"

Uncle Antonio explained that Suicide Bend was a winding stretch of track that crossed Dry Creek at the bottom of a steep grade, one that began high in the Burro Mountains. Many trains had derailed there over the years, and locomotive engineers knew enough to slow down when they reached that dangerous section of track.

"It'd be plenty easy to hop a freight train there," Uncle Antonio said. "Trains are just creeping along at that place."

"Was it the Ragland brothers?" Pablo asked. "Were Pia and Kiki with them?"

"Like I said, I can't go into detail," the FBI man said. "But we believe there is a strong probability that it was them."

"Where was the train headed?" Pablo asked, his stomach beginning to twist into a hard knot again. Pia and Kiki kidnapped. It was almost more than he could bear. Was Pia frightened? How were the Ragland brothers treating Kiki? And why would they hop a freight train? That didn't make any sense. In fact, it was the dumbest thing he had ever heard.

Something doesn't smell right about this story, Pablo thought.

"According to the railroad people, the train's ultimate destination was Little Rock, Arkansas," FBI Agent Edwards said. "It is scheduled to arrive early tomorrow. Of course, the kidnappers and their victims could easily have—"

"They have names," Pablo said stiffly. "Pia and Kiki, not victims."

"Yes, Pia Perez and Kiki Flores," the FBI man said dryly. "But as I was saying, the kidnappers could have disembarked the train at any of a number of locations. Amarillo, Texas, Oklahoma City, Oklahoma, Ft. Smith, Arkansas. We've alerted our agents between here and Little Rock to keep their eyes open. We believe they hopped the freight train because it was the last thing in the world we'd think they'd do." He flashed a conceited smile. "A little reverse psychology."

"Reverse psychology?" Helen asked skeptically.

"That's the way we have it figured," the FBI man said.

"What can we do to help?" Uncle Antonio asked, a frantic urgency in his voice. "There must be something we can do."

"I'm afraid there's not much anyone can do at this point," Agent Edwards said, taking a step toward the door. "We have your telephone number at the Bar-7, and you have my personal cell number in the event you learn something about the disposition of the victims, uh, that is Pia Perez and her cousin Kiki Flores. Now I'm afraid we have to be leaving."

"What about their horses?" Uncle Antonio said. He got up out of this chair and stepped in front of the FBI agents, blocking the doorway. "There's only one way to reach that stretch of track—by horseback. What'd the Ragland brothers do with their horses after they hopped that freight car?"

The FBI man paused to exchange a serious glimpse with the other two agents. Pablo could tell from the expression on his face that the FBI man knew more than he was telling.

In a courteous tone, Pablo said, "Please, tell us what you know about the horses, Mr. Edwards." Pablo felt the warmth of tears running down his cheek, and he quickly swiped them away with the back of his hand.

"Okay," Agent Edwards said. "Here's the story. According to Sheriff Frost, the Ragland horses had been stabled in the barn out back of the hotel. There were three horses and a mule. All four animals were gone when she inspected the barn earlier today," the FBI man said.

"That's right," Maggie Frost said, "the barn was empty. Their pickup was there, but the horses weren't. Nor the mule."

The FBI man said, "Looks like the Ragland brothers rode to the tracks at Suicide Bend, released their horses to throw us off the trail, and then hopped the next freight train."

"You think they released their horses and hopped a freight car?" Pablo asked.

"Yes," the FBI man said. "The brakeman of that freight train says he saw four riderless horses crossing the tracks near Tortilla Flat a short time after those five individuals were seen hopping the freight," the FBI agent said. "There's no doubt about it. The Ragland brothers released their horses to throw us off the trail, and then hopped that freight. They must have forced the girls to double up on one of the horses."

"Probably the mule," Sheriff Frost said.

"That's interesting," Uncle Antonio said, looking at Pablo and rolling his eyes, as if to say: "I don't believe a word of it."

Agent Edwards looked at Pablo, a serious cast to his eyes. "You're lucky you weren't sleeping in the bunkhouse last night, son. They probably would have kidnapped you, too."

"I know," Pablo said in little more than a whisper.

"Now if you'll excuse us," the FBI agent said.

The FBI man named Fred Edwards and the two other agents made a hasty exit. Pablo had several other questions he wanted to ask, but they were gone before he could get the words out.

***

A half-hour later, Uncle Antonio broke the horrible news of the kidnappings by phone to Pia and Kiki's parents back in Missouri. The parents made plans to fly into Albuquerque as quickly as possible, and Uncle Antonio said he would pick them up at the Albuquerque airport. Their plane was scheduled to arrive that evening.

Chapter 16

Consumed by a total sense of helplessness, Pablo was perched on the top rung of the corral fence, his mind filled with all sorts of dreadful thoughts. The heat of the day was stifling, but Pablo didn't notice. He gazed at the snowy peaks of the Burro Mountains and wondered how best to rescue his sister and cousin. The chiseled, distant peaks seemed to beckon him.

"But where do I start?" he whispered. "Where?"

A loud voice suddenly broke Pablo's train of thought.

"Dago Te!"

Pablo nearly fell off the fence.

"Dago Te!" Pablo replied, his daydream coming to an abrupt end, his breath hitching in his throat, as it always did when Charlie Pecos announced his presence. One moment Charlie Pecos was nowhere to be seen, and the next he was standing not ten feet away.

"I know about your sister and cousin," Charlie said. "It is a bad thing, this kidnapping."

"I feel helpless, Charlie," Pablo said gloomily. "I want to rescue Pia and Kiki, but I don't know where to start. I don't think there's much I can do. It's sort of out of my hands."

"You are wrong, Pablo Perez. There is much that you can do," Charlie said, his Apache eyes smiling.

"Pia and her kidnappers are probably somewhere in Texas by now," Pablo said. "The FBI said five people hopped a freight train at Suicide Bend. They think it was Pia and Kiki and three of the Ragland brothers. It doesn't make much sense to me, if you want to know the truth."

"The men calling themselves FBI are right," Charlie said. "Five people did climb aboard a freight train this morning at Suicide Bend, but it was not your sister and cousin. It was not their kidnappers."

"It wasn't?" Pablo said, surprise in his voice. "Who then?"

"Mexicans," Charlie said, a twinkle in his dark, kind eyes.

"Mexicans?"

"Undocumented workers," Charlie Pecos said. "They are headed for Arkansas and work in the poultry plants. They crossed the border near Las Cruces, New Mexico, and walked for three days before hopping a ride on that freight train headed east."

"But the engineer of that train told the FBI he saw four riderless horses crossing the tracks near Tortilla Flat."

Charlie smiled. "Yes, a small herd of horses did cross the tracks this morning near Tortilla Flat," Charlie explained. "But there were nine horses in the herd. The engineer saw only the last four. And it was not the horses belonging to the Ragland brothers."

"No?"

"It was part of the wild herd that roams Bar-7 land," Charlie said. "It was part of the herd that Moses once belonged to."

"Then where are the Ragland brothers?" Pablo asked, the knot beginning to tighten in his stomach again. "Where are Pia and Kiki?"

"The Ragland brothers rode into the Burro Mountains on three horses and a mule," Charlie said. "Young Pia and Kiki rode the mule."

Pablo paused, thinking. "Where are they headed, Charlie? And what will they do once they get there?" Pablo had a sick feeling he knew the answer to his last question, and for a moment he almost wished they had never started documenting the rock drawings. The kidnapping was all about documenting the glyphs. "And how do you...how do you know all of this?"

Charlie grinned. "There is an old Indian saying: 'Dreams are wiser than men.' I saw this dream in my mind. It is a gift from God."

Pablo didn't want the details. It seemed too fantastic. It

seemed like a bunch of Native American nonsense. But still...And what about the dream he'd had? An Apache chief had come to him in a dream and warned him. The dream had proven to be true. Pablo remembered what he had told Pia and Kiki: "There is a lot about the world we don't understand."

Pablo paused again, and then said, "But why would the Ragland brothers escape to the Burro Mountains with Pia and Kiki? That seems lame."

"These men act before they think," Charlie said. "There are many old mines in those mountains. Long tunnels and deep holes." Charlie paused. "Do you understand what I mean when I say deep holes?"

"You mean the Raglands are planning to drop my sister and cousin—?" He couldn't bring himself to finish the thought.

"Yes, Pablo. There will be no witnesses to their crime," Charlie said. "They know the mountain and the mines. They once spent a summer panning for silver in Dry Creek, which runs down the mountain near the abandoned Jane Sloan Mine. They found no silver, only hard work. They have a distaste for hard work."

A flood of adrenaline rushed through Pablo's veins. Pia and Kiki weren't on a train headed to Arkansas. They were twenty miles away in the Burro Mountains. There *was* something he could do after all. He *could* rescue his sister and cousin, but there was no time to lose.

"What should we do, Charlie?"

"Saddle up."

Chapter 17

It was a little after two that afternoon when Pablo and Charlie reached the deserted mining town of Axe Handle. They had made the hot, fifteen-mile ride along Dry Creek in less than two hours, Pablo aboard his brown and white Paint named Buster, and Charlie atop the Mustang he called Moses. Sampson the Wonder Dog had joined in the rescue attempt, barking and frolicking most of the way. Pablo was amazed at Sampson's speed and stamina.

Charlie insisted that Pablo remain in the saddle while he searched the Silver Nugget Hotel. Not surprisingly, the Apache cowboy found the hotel deserted. Indeed, nothing had changed since Maggie Frost and her deputy had searched the place earlier in the day.

Pablo and Charlie rode around to the old horse barn, which was located behind the abandoned hotel. Sampson immediately picked up the trail left by the three horses and a mule. The tracks headed west out of Axe Handle toward the Burro Mountains along Dry Creek.

Charlie dismounted and knelt beside the hoof prints.

"When did they leave, Charlie?" Pablo asked, looking down at the tracks. "Can you tell from the prints?"

The Mescalero Apache ran his finger lightly over the indentations. "They are not fresh. The wind has deposited many hours of dirt into the tracks. They were made early this morning. No later than sunrise."

Pablo nodded. That timeline seemed to fit. Sheriff Frost and her deputy had been there about ten that morning to find the Ragland brothers gone.

"If they kidnapped Pia and Kiki around three o'clock in the morning, and then returned to Axe Handle to swap their pickup for horses, why did they wait until sunrise to leave?"

"I cannot answer that question," Charlie replied.

"But you have the gift—"

"There are many things I can't see."

The Raglands' 1965 Chevy pickup truck was parked outside the barn, and Charlie climbed into the bed of the truck, which was filled with trash. He found a gunnysack (one of the sacks the Raglands had used to transport the stolen glyphs) which he cut into one long strip with his pocketknife. He climbed down, unscrewed the truck's gasoline cap, and stuffed one end of the burlap sack into the opening. He shoved the burlap strip deep into the gasoline tank with the long handle of a broken pitchfork that he found in the barn. He left the other end of the sack hanging from the gas tank.

Charlie looked up at Pablo, who by now had figured out what the Apache cowboy was up to. "If the Raglands double back," Charlie said, "they will not have the luxury of a pick-up."

Pablo nodded his understanding.

"Do not try this at home," Charlie grinned.

"You can bet on it," Pablo said.

"Be ready to ride."

Pablo grasped the reins firmly in his hands. Buster seemed to sense the tension in Pablo's legs, and the big stallion tossed his head back with a whinny and a snort.

Charlie removed a small box of wooden matches from his pocket, lit the flagging end of the burlap cloth, and then hurried over to Moses. He leaped into the saddle with the agility of a circus performer, and he and Pablo galloped out of town.

They had reached the edge of Axe Handle when the old pickup exploded in a clamorous ball of fire. Turning in the saddle, Pablo watched a thirty-foot fireball dance into the afternoon sky above the silhouette of deserted buildings.

***

With Charlie's three-legged dog in the lead, they followed the four sets of hoof prints out of Axe Handle, west along Dry Creek, and into the foothills of the Burro Mountains.

They rode along a well-worn animal trail that ran

parallel to Dry Creek. It climbed the foothills, twisting and turning upward. Leaving the arid prairie, the trail continued to climb and soon crossed an old mining road, one which bisected heavy stands of juniper and oak. Although the road was overgrown with vegetation, the hoof prints were easy to follow in the soft soil.

Quite unexpectedly, all four sets of tracks made a sharp ninety-degree turn toward the north and through a patch of oak trees.

"Where are they headed?" Pablo asked.

Charlie shook his head, but said nothing.

They followed the hoof prints, which continued north for a hundred yards or so, weaving in and out of the trees before making a circle and returning to the mining road.

"What was that all about?" Pablo asked, perplexed, staring down at the hoof prints.

"Pia and Kiki tried to escape," Charlie replied. "But their mule was too slow."

The thought of his sister and cousin trying to escape tightened the knot in Pablo's stomach. *When I find that Red Ragland...* he thought angrily.

They rode on.

***

Several times during the slow pursuit, Moses whinnied restlessly and reared up on his hind legs. Pablo thought Moses had sensed the presence of a wild animal—a mountain lion, perhaps—but Charlie explained the Mustang's stormy behavior.

"Moses smells his wild herd. They come to the mountains during the heat of the day for water," the Apache man said. "Moses still longs to be free."

They had spotted the Mustangs earlier racing through the forest. Pablo marveled at the speed and grace of the herd, which melted quickly into the heavy timber.

They stopped about five that afternoon and allowed their horses to drink from a small pool of water. There were numerous hoof prints around the mountain pond, and Charlie said the wild herd had been there earlier.

Even though the water had a strange taste, Charlie said it was okay to drink, and they filled their canteens. Pablo's canteen was almost empty. Sampson frolicked like a child, running through the pool and snapping at the splashing water.

***

The air began to cool as they rode higher and deeper into the Burro Mountains, and at a point where the valley narrowed, the mining road crossed Dry Creek, which was now supported by a thin trickle of live water.

Above them, peering down from both sides of the valley walls, were the black mouths of mine entrances. The dark holes gave Pablo an uncomfortable feeling. It was almost as if the mountain had eyes and was watching them.

"Hundreds of miners once worked these mountains," Charlie Pecos said, staring into the porous hillsides. "Many died having never seen a single flake of silver."

They continued on, Sampson the Wonder Dog leading the way, his nose to the ground.

At a place where the terrain around the river flattened, two sets of hoof prints led away from the riverbank. The strides were long and Charlie said the two animals were running—the mule and a horse. They led into the forest for a short distance, and then returned to the river.

"Again, Pia and Kiki have tried to escape on their mule," Charlie Pecos said solemnly, waving a finger at the hoof prints.

"Pia and Kiki are strong," Pablo told Charlie, putting words to the thread of his thoughts. "They wouldn't give up without a fight."

***

Fifteen minutes later, Charlie said, "Finally, they show some sense." He was looking down at the four sets of hoof prints they had been following all day. The hoof prints led into Dry Creek, which had grown from a tickle of water to a shallow, but well-defined stream.

"What do you mean, Charlie?"

"I mean, no passing is recorded by Mother Stream," Charlie Pecos said. "Hoof prints are washed away in the water."

"Then how will we follow them?"

"The Raglands think they are fooling us with this amateur display of hide and seek, but I know where they are headed."

"You do?"

Charlie nodded. "The Jane Sloan Mine." He raised a finger. "Higher up the mountain at a place where the brothers once panned for silver. They know that place, and they are comfortable there."

They rode on, and in a few minutes, partially hidden by tall evergreen on all sides, they came upon a large wooden structure. It reminded Pablo of a medieval castle—old and forbidding. As they approached, Pablo could make out a sign near the main entrance. It read in faded black letters: **JANE SLOAN MINE MUSEUM.**

The dilapidated structure was covered with a rusty tin roof. Charlie said it had once been a processing plant, a place where the silver ore was crushed and treated. The building was later turned into a museum.

The two-story building leaned to one side to such an extent that it appeared as if it might collapse at any moment. Most of the windows had been boarded shut. Vegetation grew up the outside walls, and many of the tin roof panels were missing. A tall, red-brick chimney ascended from the center of the building. Large piles of chat—many rose more than a hundred feet—occupied spaces along one side of the structure.

Pablo spied two sets of thin, narrow-gauge railroad tracks in the tall grass at the rear of the building. The tracks extended up the mountain, running parallel to the obscure mining road they had been following.

Charlie motioned toward the railroad tracks. "One set of tracks were used to bring the ore down the mountain, and the other took the empty ore wagons back up."

An elevated wooden trestle that had once connected the tracks to the second story of the building had collapsed, and an empty space of thirty feet or so now existed between the ends of the rails and the building.

"The tracks will take us to the mine," Charlie explained. "It's about four miles ahead."

"The Raglands are taking Pia and Kiki to the mine?" Pablo asked in a quiet voice, a disturbing image taking shape in his mind.

Charlie nodded grimly. "Yes."

Several more gruesome thoughts clawed their way into Pablo's mind, but he quickly pushed them away.

Charlie pointed out a row of small cottages set back in the forest not far from the abandoned ore processing plant. He said the miners lived in the small houses, sometimes four or five to a room. The cottages were in the final stages of collapsing decay, and only one supported a roof.

"Hard-rock silver mining was not easy work," Charlie said. "Many men died in the mines."

Pablo asked about the ore plant turned museum.

Charlie laughed softly. "A man from Albuquerque had the idea of making the abandoned processing plant a museum, and for a short spell—I think back in the sixties—it was open for business. It didn't last long. It is too far up the mountain for people to drive. There once was a road, which has been reclaimed by Mother Nature."

They continued up the mountain, riding alongside the narrow-gauge tracks.

***

The long, cold shadows of evening fell over the forest when a cottontail rabbit darted out of the bushes and hurried into the forest. Charlie reined in Moses, and said, "We'll rest here for a time, Pablo."

"Rest?" Pablo blurted out. "Shouldn't we go on?" Pablo didn't want to stop until they had reached the mine and rescued Pia and Kiki. There was no time to lose.

"It is too dangerous at night. We need the light of day to rescue your sister and cousin. It will be dark by the time we reach them. We will locate their camp tonight, but a rescue must wait until daybreak."

"I don't care if it's dangerous or not, Charlie," Pablo said, anger bubbling up inside him. "I say we find them, the sooner, the better." Pablo was breathing heavy. He didn't know if it was the altitude or his anger that was making him breathe so hard.

"We must wait until dawn to make good the rescue," Charlie insisted. "The girls are safe for the moment. No harm will come to them this night."

"But how can you be so sure?"

"They have made camp at the mine, and Pia and Kiki are safe," Charlie repeated.

Pablo sighed. "I hope you're right, Charlie."

"We must rest the horses before we attempt the rescue. There is an old Indian saying: 'Dead horses are good for nothing but eating.'"

Pablo grimaced. The thought of eating a horse was not very appetizing.

"Our horses must rest, then we will find the Raglands and their campfire, but a rescue will not come tonight."

Pablo didn't want to admit it, but Charlie was probably right. Rushing in with a half-baked plan might backfire.

They tied Buster and Moses to a tree next to Dry Creek, which allowed their mounts to drink. Sampson found a shallow hole of water and lay in it.

Before leaving the Bar-7, Charlie said they would make better time if they traveled light—water only, no food—and

Pablo's stomach was empty with pain. He hadn't eaten all day. It had been rumbling and grumbling for the past hour, and he didn't know if the source of his pain was the kidnapping or hunger. He decided it was a little of both.

Charlie removed an odd-looking stick from his saddlebag. The stick resembled a boomerang.

"Build a fire, Pablo," Charlie said, tossing him a small box of wooden matches. "We will leave the horses saddled for the night. I'll return soon."

Before Pablo could say another word, Charlie disappeared into the forest gloom, Sampson at his heels.

Pablo gathered an armload of dead limbs from the surrounding forest and built a small fire in an open patch of ground near the stream. The worrisome thought continued to torment him: *If I had stayed in the bunkhouse, none of his would have happened.*

Off to the north, beyond the lofty, snow splattered peaks of the Burro Mountains, a flash of lightning illuminated the evening sky.

In a few minutes, Charlie Pecos returned. He was carrying a dead rabbit in one hand and the odd-shaped stick in the other.

"Dinner," Charlie said, smiling and placing the curved stick in his back pocket. "I thanked Mr. Rabbit for giving his life to us. He was a noble beast. He said he was glad to help."

After cleaning the rabbit, Charlie impaled the fleshy carcass on a sharp stick and roasted it over the fire.

"There is an old Indian saying: 'Before eating, always take a little time to thank the food.'"

Charlie said a short prayer, and then divided the rabbit meat with Pablo.

Pablo ate with his hands, and couldn't remember anything ever tasting so good.

"What's with that curved stick in your pocket?" Pablo said a few minutes later. He was lying on his bedroll near the fire.

"It is called a rabbit stick," Charlie said.

Pablo chuckled. "A rabbit stick? Where'd it get its name?"

"It is used to killed rabbits. My people have used them for generations." Charlie removed the strange looking weapon from his back pocket. "It is thrown like this." He held the curved stick by one end. "I use it only for food. It is very accurate."

As the murky shadows of night stretched over their campsite, Charlie demonstrated the proper use of the rabbit stick. Standing back a short distance from a pine tree, Charlie drew back his arm and then hurled the curved stick. It swished through the air, striking a tree limb and breaking it in half.

"Wow!" Pablo gasped. "Can I try?"

Charlie showed Pablo how to hold the stick and how best to hurl it.

"You must hold it gently. Do not squeeze. Grip it as you might grip the hand of a woman. Grip it tenderly."

Pablo's first throws were erratic and missed the tree completely. The heavy, foot-long stick had a tendency to curve to the left and Pablo had to allow for the arc. After a couple of dozen tries he began to get the hang of it. Limbs snapped with every throw.

Charlie said Pablo could keep the rabbit stick. "I have others."

Chapter 18

"You said it'd get better, Red!" Gordo cried. "But it ain't getting better! It's getting worse!" Gordo was seated by the fire, his pants leg rolled up to his knee. His leg was draped over his saddle. From the knee down, Gordo's leg was swollen to the size of his meaty thigh. The skin was a jumble of nauseous colors, mostly reds, and covered with blisters, some the size of golf balls. "I tell you it ain't getting better, Red, it's getting worse!" Gordo's face was twisted in pain.

"Ya done said that," Red barked. "Why'd ya have to go and get yourself snake bit?" Red was eating a cold can of beans.

"Bad timing," Gordo moaned.

"You're an idiot," Red muttered.

The Ragland brothers were huddled around a campfire a few yards from the entrance to a mine entrance. A faded sign over the tunnel entrance identified it: **Jane Sloan Mine #2.** The three brothers had unsaddled their horses and mule, and tied them to a rusting ore cart that was leaning against a nearby shack, one of three small structures that had been built decades before on the dirt landing. Rusty, worthless mining equipment of all shapes and sizes littered the landing.

The flames from the campfire reflected ghoulish figures off the rotting walls of the shack.

The door was lettered in faded white paint:

JANE SLOAN MINE
EMPLOYMENT OFFICE

In smaller letters were the words:

APPLY FOR WORK HERE
LEAVE YOUR FIREARMS OUTSIDE

Unharmed, but afraid, Pia and Kiki were wrapped in one another's embrace inside the wooden shed. Pirate had given Pia his poncho and Kiki his jacket. At an altitude of more than eight thousand feet, the air had cooled the minute the sun had set.

The door to the wooden hut had been off kilter, and Red had muscled it into position, and then wedged a heavy railroad tie against the door to keep it closed and his prisoners inside. The shack's two windows had been boarded shut decades earlier.

Many of the silver mines gouged into the side of Burro Mountain had been dug by hand, mostly with pick and shovel by hard-rock miners, and most tunnels didn't extend more than a few dozen feet into the mountainside.

Other tunnels, however, had been the prize of big mining outfits like the Jane Sloan Mining Company of Denver, Colorado. They had conquered the mountain with steam drills and explosives, and these tunnels extended deep into Burro Mountain, some for more than a mile. Many of these tunnels were pitted with deep shafts, and most had filled with water over the years.

Ever since they had arrived at the mine site—indeed, ever since their encounter with the Diamondback rattler the night before—Gordo had moaned and groaned, and complained mightily that his miserable life was nothing more than one episode of bad timing followed by another.

"Just don't put no weight on that leg," Pirate suggested, feeding limbs to the fire. "Sometimes a snake bite will heal itself." Pirate had wrapped himself in his horse blanket.

In a loud, moaning voice, Gordo said, "I'm snake bit and my own brothers is watching me die!"

"Are we gonna hear ya carry on like that all night?" Red asked with mild indifference. "Ya complained all day, now you're fixing to complain all night."

"It hurts something awful, Red!" Gordon cried. "I can't hardly stand the pain."

Gordo had been bitten by the Diamondback during the early-morning kidnapping of Pia and Kiki. Coiled in one corner of the girls' bunkhouse bedroom, the deadly viper had found a warm, cozy corner and had just given birth to a dozen baby rattlers when Red and Gordo crept into the room. Pirate was the getaway driver, and he had waited in the pickup truck.

Using her infrared detectors to locate her warm-blooded prey in total darkness—and intent on protecting her babies—the mother snake had struck the first warm image that appeared: Gordo's leg.

At first, it was thought the snake had done little damage. Located a few inches above the top of Gordo's boot, the snake's deadly fangs had penetrated his pants. The two tiny wounds appeared to be nothing more than small scratches. By the time they arrived back at Axe Handle to exchange the pickup for horses, however, Gordo's leg had started to swell and the pain had found a home.

Gordo's misfortune had distracted Red and Pirate, and they had lost nearly two hours of valuable time trying to find Pia and Kiki, who had escaped into the hotel attic. The three brothers and their hostages hadn't left Axe Handle until dawn.

"Why is it me with all the bad luck, all the bad timing?" Gordo moaned bitterly, his eyes riveted on the grotesque blisters on his leg. "It ain't fair."

"Shut your trap!" Red warned, staring into the campfire. "I'm trying to think."

Sipping on a cup of instant coffee, the one-eyed Ragland brother looked across the campfire at Red. "I reckon it's about two hundred yards."

Perplexed, Red looked up. "Huh?"

"You're trying to remember how far back a body has to walk to get to that there deep shaft," Pirate said. "It's about two hundred yards from the entrance."

"Yeah, right, two hundred yards. Maybe we should check it out. Maybe it's full of water all the way to the top. It ain't no good if it's full of water all the way to the top."

"Go on ahead," Pirate said, waving a finger at the coal-black entrance to the mine. "Be my guest. The last time I was in that tunnel I saw the way them overhead beams was bowing. That ceiling ain't safe. A man breathe real hard and that ceiling is sure enough coming down."

"If the ceiling was gonna fall, it seems to me it would have already did so," Red argued.

"Maybe," Pirate said, sipping his coffee. "I'm all whipped. A long day in the saddle. Be my guest. Go check it out."

Red gazed at the tunnel entrance. The campfire casting eerie, flickering shadows on the rocky entry, it resembled the open mouth of a wild beast.

"We'll check it out in the morning. Ain't got no legs neither," Red claimed. "I'm plum tuckered out myself."

"What about me?" Gordo wailed, his suffering written all over his round, plump face. "I might be dead by morning."

In a girlish, mocking voice, Red said, "I might be dead by morning."

"It hurts something awful!"

At the end of his patience, Red retrieved a bottle of whiskey from his saddlebag and gave it to his snake-bit brother. Gordo drank the liquor straight from the bottle, tipping the half-full container several times until it was empty.

***

The alcohol had helped deaden Gordo's pain, and in a few minutes, he was asleep.

Pirate got up and threw a few limbs into the fire, and said in a somber tone, "This here kidnapping is serious business, Red, and I ain't liking it one bit."

"How can they say we kidnapped them gals if there ain't no bodies?" He grinned foolishly. "No bodies, no kidnapping."

"I reckon you know there's blackdamp in that there mine tunnel," Pirate pointed out.

"Black what?" Red said, sending a stream of brownish tobacco juice onto the ground.

"Blackdamp. No air."

"Ain't no air? Bro, there's air everywheres...except maybe on the moon."

"Bad ceiling and blackdamp. Ain't safe."

"Since when was you an expert about mines?"

"I'm telling you, it ain't safe."

***

Inside the shack, Pia and Kiki were seated on the floor, their backs against a wall. They were in pajamas and socks. It was the same pajamas and socks they were wearing when they had been abducted. They were holding hands, and trying very hard to hear the Ragland brothers' conversation. Although most of the words had a fuzzy, hollow sound, Pia and Kiki had distinctly heard Red's earlier comment: "How can they say we kidnapped them gals if there ain't no bodies? No bodies, no kidnapping." The comment had caused them to tremble with fear.

"Where's Pablo?" Pia asked for the umpteenth time, crowding in closer to Kiki.

"He'll be here," Kiki said confidently.

"I can feel my heart beating," Pia said in a breathy voice, her hand on her chest.

Her expression grave, Kiki nodded. "I know. My heart's beating really hard, too." Kiki wrapped her arm around Pia. "Let's try and get some sleep. Nothing is going to happen tonight."

"What if Pablo doesn't come?"

"He'll come."

"Are you just saying that or do you really mean it?"

"I really mean it."

***

Leading their horses by the reins, Pablo and Charlie Pecos crept quietly through the forest. The Ragland's campfire was visible a hundred yards or so ahead through the heavy timber. Off to their right, like a lion stalking its prey, Sampson the Wonder Dog likewise moved silently through the forest.

Pablo tied Buster to a tree and Charlie hobbled Moses. Then they continued up the mountain until they reached a thick grove of Aspen, which was growing at the edge of the dirt landing. Off to their right was the narrow-gauge tracks once used by the miners to transport the ore down the mountain to the processing plant. Pablo and Charlie knelt, their eyes focused on the three figures crowded together around the fire on the far side of the landing near the entrance to the mine.

"Where's Pia and Kiki?" Pablo whispered. "I don't see them."

"The shack," Charlie said, leveling a finger at the rotting hut. "The Raglands have wedged a railroad tie against the door. Pia and Kiki are prisoners in the shack."

Pablo breathed a sigh of relief. His sister and cousin were still alive. Weren't they? "Are you sure, Charlie?"

Charlie's eyes fell shut. In a few moments he nodded. "They are in the shack. They are unhurt."

"You...you saw them?" Pablo asked, still wrestling with Charlie's claim for seeing things from afar.

Charlie nodded. "It is a gift."

In a quiet voice, Pablo said, "I can circle around to the right and come in from—"

"Patience, Pablo Perez," Charlie advised.

"We can do it, Charlie. It'll be simple. You get their attention, and while they're focused on you, I'll sneak in, knock that railroad tie away from the door, and rescue Pia and Kiki."

"There is an old Indian saying: 'Show patience and eventually your enemy will trip.'"

"How are they going to...trip?"

"We will watch and see. Besides, they have rifles, we have only our rabbit sticks."

But Pablo was persistent. "Maybe after everyone's asleep we could..." In the moonlight, Pablo read the stern expression on Charlie's face, and he nodded. "Okay, patience."

"We will sleep here for the night. In the morning, we will see if the Raglands trip."

Chapter 19

Pirate was the first one up the following morning, and he walked over to the shack, pushed the railroad tie away from the door and went inside. Pia and Kiki were huddled together in a corner of the one-room shack, their eyes filled with fear.

"You little gals sleep okay?" Pirate asked pleasantly.

"What do you think?" Kiki replied curtly. She rubbed the sleep from her eyes.

"I'm thinking you probably slept about as well as I did," Pirate said.

"Yes, I suppose you're right," Kiki said. "Thanks for the poncho and jacket. Weren't you cold?"

"I had me a big old saddle blanket. It was right warm."

"What are you going to do with us?" Pia asked in a pleading voice, a sob lodged in her throat.

"It ain't my decision to make, little gal," Pirate said. "Either of you drink coffee? I'm warming water for instant coffee. Sorry, ain't got nothing to eat. Red done ate all the beans."

"We'll pass," Kiki said.

Pirate looked at Pia and smiled. "I seen you in the canyon that day sketching them rocks and all. You like to sketch?"

"I'm not very good," Pia replied hesitantly. "But it's… it's sort of fun."

"Me, too. I like to sketch things. The sky. The mountains. Even that there canyon." Pirate flashed a boyish grin. "That's my favorite thing in the world to sketch—Petroglyph Canyon."

"I'd like to see your sketches sometime," Kiki said, appealing to Pirate's gentle nature. "Do you happen to have any—"

From outside the shack came an anguished cry: "My leg hurts something awful!"

Looking at Pia and Kiki, Pirate said, "Guess I'd better be tending to my brother. I reckon I'll see you little gals directly"

"Pirate, it doesn't have to be this way," Kiki said glumly. "You seem like a nice person. Throwing us down a hole is only going to make things worse for you."

Pirate paused, started to speak, paused again, and then said: "Ain't my decision, little gal." He walked out the door, leaving it ajar.

Outside, Pirate went over to where his snake-bit brother was lying. Although the swelling had gone down, Gordo's blistered leg had turned a nasty shade of black. Pirate offered to clean his brother's leg with warm water, but Gordo would have none of it.

"Don't want ya touching it," Gordo moaned. "Hurts something terrible to touch it."

Red had been awakened by Gordo's painful outburst, and he had already loaded his mouth with a huge chaw of tobacco. It was a morning ritual. He spit a stream of juice into the embers of the fire, and then said: "Now ya listen to me, Gordo, and ya listen good. I don't want ya slowing me down none today. As long as ya can sit in a saddle, me and you is going to git along just fine."

"It hurts something awful, Red," Gordo groaned. Drawing a painful breath, he said: "But I'll give 'er a try."

"Trying ain't good enough," Red snarled. "There's gonna be lawmen looking to tan our hides. We do the dirty deed, then we gotta ride—hard and fast."

"Shoulda cut that boot off," Pirate said, sitting astride his saddle and sipping his coffee. "That foot is hurting 'cause it ain't got no place to swell. Should of cut that boot off. Still can, if you're up to it, Gordo."

"Ain't cutting my boot off," Gordo protested. "How can I ride without no boot?"

Pirate blew on his steaming coffee and nodded. "I reckon you're right."

"Maybe a cup of...cup of coffee will get me going," Gordo said.

Pirate prepared a cup of instant coffee for his snake-bit brother, and took it to him.

"Thanks, bro," Gordo said, bringing the hot cup up to his nose. He looked at Pirate with a thankful but pained smile. "Smells good."

Red had suddenly grown impatient, and he said: "We're wasting time. John Law's sure enough on our tail by now. We gotta do the dirty deed and ride." He turned toward the shack, and in a loud voice said, "You little gals in the shack, come on out!"

In a few seconds, Kiki pushed the door open and she and Pia appeared.

"Come on over by the fire," Red offered, waving them closer.

Hesitantly, Pia and Kiki stepped out of the shack, and came over and stood near the fire. Pia was blinking like a lizard.

"Good morning, little gals," Red said in a cheerful but menacing voice.

"What's good about it?" Kiki replied, summoning all her bluster. Sleeping on the hard wooden floor had made her bones stiff, and she twisted and arched her back.

"Yeah, what's good about it?" Pia said, a slight quiver of alarm in her voice. She grasped Kiki's hand and put on a brave face.

"This here's your special day," Red grinned. "Fact is, this here is the most special day of your lives." When there was no reply from his two captives, Red said, "Ain't ya gonna ask me why?"

"I think we know why, Henry," Kiki snapped.

Angry laughter slipped over Red Ragland's thin lips, and he spit into the fire. It made a hissing sound. "We can do this the easy way or the hard way. Up to you little gals. Easy or hard. First, ya tried to make a call on your cell phone—"

"Text, not call," Kiki corrected assertively. "And I'm pretty sure my cousin Pablo received it loud and clear."

"Whatever," Red said with a dismissive wave of his hand. "Then ya run off and hid in the hotel attic, and we lost some valuable time. Then ya tried to ride off twice on the way up here, and now I'm getting a little tired of running after ya. The fun and games is over."

Pia tightened her grip on Kiki's hand.

His cruel mind sorting through God-only-knew-what, Red stared at his two captives for several long moments. Finally, he told Pirate, "Git it done, bro, and git it done before I've finished my second cup of your rot-gut coffee."

A soft ripple of thunder swept over the mountain, and

Gordo glanced up at the morning sky, which was beginning to darken.

"Bad timing," Gordo said warily, staring up at the black-board sky, the pain in his leg forgotten for the moment. In little more than a whisper—it was doubtful that either of his brothers could hear him—Gordo said, "Something bad is coming...."

Pirate looked at Red with a surprised expression. "I thought you was going to do the dirty deed, Red?"

"Changed my mine," Red growled, waving a finger at the entrance to the mine. "Now, git 'er done."

***

Pablo and Charlie had been watching the drama unfold from their hiding place at the edge of the forest, fifty yards away. They had slept on the cold ground, and Pablo was rubbing his hands to warm them as he watched, his puckish stomach feeling like he had swallowed a dozen live worms.

Pablo observed attentively as Pirate led his sister and cousin up the slight incline and into the mouth of the mining tunnel. Pia, Kiki, and Pirate followed the narrow-gauge rails that extended into the tunnel. The darkness beyond entrance quickly swallowed them.

"We can't wait any longer, Charlie!" Pablo said in a hushed voice, jumping to his feet. "It's now or never!"

Charlie Pecos grabbed Pablo by the sleeve of his jacket and pulled him to the ground. "Wait, Pablo Perez!"

"Charlie…!"

In a calm voice, Charlie said, "You must trust me, Pablo. You must trust me like you have never trusted anyone in your life."

"I'm trying, Charlie," Pablo said, quietly marking time, his eyes riveted on the dark mouth of the tunnel, the slithery worms crawling up and down the walls of his stomach. "I'm trying real hard, but my sister, my cousin. They need me."

"Patience."

Pablo heaved an impatient sigh. "Patience."

Five seconds elapsed. Then ten. Twenty seconds passed, and then thirty.

"Charlie! When?"

It had been almost two full minutes when a muffled scream spewed forth from the tunnel and across the landing to where Pablo and Charlie were crouched in the forest.

That was Kiki!

"Charlie!" Pablo cried, again climbing to his feet. "It's… it's…"

"Wait! Listen!"

In the next second there was a second muffled scream.

"It's Pia!" Pablo whispered. It was all he could do not to shout his sister's name. The worms were beginning to eat his guts.

Charlie Pecos closed his eyes, his mind a million miles away.

In a moment, the Apache cowboy opened his eyes and in a calm voice said, "Pirate will not harm them."

Pablo was speechless.

"Didn't you hear?" Charlie said, looking up at Pablo, his expression oddly serene.

"Yes, Charlie, I heard! Kiki and Pia screamed!" Why was Charlie so relaxed? It didn't make any sense. Pia and Kiki had screamed in terror.

"And...?"

Pablo gave it more thought. There was something odd about Kiki's scream. And Pia's, for that matter. What was it that sounded so odd?

Then it came to Pablo.

"Charlie, it didn't sound real. It sounded fake. Was it fake?"

Charlie Pecos nodded with a smile.

***

Pia and Kiki stood at the edge of the deep hole, their fake screams still echoing throughout the many dark chambers of the Jane Sloan Mine #2. The gaping hole before them had been carved into the belly of the mountain a hundred years earlier by miners following a rich vein of silver ore, and twenty feet below was a pool of water. It reflected tiny gems of light from Pirate's flashlight.

Pirate had devised a plan to spare Pia and Kiki from a watery grave. The first part of the plan had worked perfectly. Red had taken the bait—Pirate had convinced him that the mine was not safe—and in the end Red had insisted that Pirate do "the dirty deed."

"Great screams, little gals," Pirate said, directing the beam from his flashlight up from the pool of water and onto them.

"Now what?" Kiki asked, her voice trembling with doubt. Pirate hadn't shared his plan with them until they had reached the shaft, and Pia and Kiki were still terrified. Kiki knew they weren't out of the woods yet. Far from it.

"I done tricked my brother into thinking this here mine was a dangerous place." Pirate grinned in the darkness. "He ain't all that smart."

"What's the rest of your plan, Pirate?" Kiki said urgently. "There is more to your plan, right?"

Pirate motioned to an empty ore cart setting on the narrow-gauge rails a few yards away. "Climb in."

"Inside the ore cart?" Kiki asked, surprised.

"Yes, and you little gals keep your heads down and don't be talking. Got to stay quiet."

The three of them hurried over to the ore wagon, and Pirate lifted Pia then Kiki into it. The decaying old relic was about the size of a carnival ride. The rusty iron wheels were perched precariously on the corroded rails. The floor of the buggy was littered with rocky fragments of ore.

"Stay put," Pirate said in a low voice. "Don't you be coming out for at least an hour," he warned. "We'll sure enough be gone by then. You're on your own after that. Follow Dry Creek down the mountain. It'll sure enough take you back to the ranch."

Kiki took Pirate by the hand and squeezed it. "Thank you, Pirate...for everything."

"Yes, thank you, thank you," Pia said, her eyes glistening with tears.

"Can't abide by killing little gals." He adjusted his dark eye patch. "It just ain't right." He started to turn and leave, but paused. "Remember now, at least an hour."

"Pirate," Pia said, "I'd like to see your sketches some-day. I'll bet they're pretty cool."

Pirate smiled. "And I'd like to see your sketches, little gal. I'll bet they're pretty cool, too." Pirate then turned and hurried toward the dim speck of light in the distance.

***

"What now?" Pablo asked, his eyes fixed on Pirate as he emerged from the mining tunnel.

"Patience, Pablo Perez."

"Let's mount up and ride right into the tunnel. Ride in

and double up on Buster and Moses. You get Kiki and I'll get Pia, and then ride like heck." Pablo paused. "They're still alive, right? You're sure those were fake screams?"

Charlie closed his eyes for a moment, and then said, "Yes, they are fine. They are hiding in an ore wagon, but it still too dangerous to ride in. We must wait. The Ragland brothers have guns. We have only our rabbit sticks. We must wait until the Ragland brothers are gone, then we will ride in and rescue your sister and cousin."

**

"Did ya do the dirty deed?" Red asked Pirate as the one-eyed cowboy strolled over to the fire and made himself another cup of coffee. The handle of the pan was hot, and he poured the water quickly into his cup and set the pan back on the fire. He added instant coffee from the jar and stirred it with a small stick.

"Yep, did the dirty deed," Pirate replied. "Not a pretty sight, but I got 'er done."

"It hurts something awful," Gordo groaned softly.

Pirate glanced at his overweight brother, who had rolled his pants leg down and was seated cockeyed atop his saddle. "How's the leg?"

"She still hurts something terrible," Gordo replied with a pained smile. "But I reckon I can ride."

"That there shaft still holding water?" Red sat on his

haunches before the fire. He rotated his head slightly and looked up at Pirate suspiciously.

"Yep. Still holding water."

"How's come I didn't hear no splash?"

"Did you hear the screams?" Pirate sipped his coffee, not the slightly sign of worry on his face.

"Heard them screams, but not the splashes." Red definitely smelled a rat.

"There was splashes. Two splashes. Hole's deep. Besides, them little gals didn't make much of a splash. I barely heard it myself." Pirate sipped his coffee without a care in the world.

"I didn't hear no splashes," Red repeated, his beady eyes filled with mistrust.

"Go on in and check for yourself. They was treading water when I left," Pirate said in a relaxed tone of voice. "The little one couldn't barely hold her head above the water. Pretty sad sight. They can't tread water forever."

"Maybe I'll check and see if my one-eyed brother is lying."

"Ain't lying. Go on ahead. Be my guest," Pirate said with a poker face.

Red stood up. "Maybe I'll do just—"

Red turned his eyes skyward as the faraway whirl of helicopter blades beat the thin mountain air. In few seconds

Truman Hathaway's Bell 407 appeared, skimming above the treetops.

"What's he doing here? Gordo asked, staring at the sleek aircraft.

"He's making sure the dirty deed got gone," Red advised, giving Hathaway a wave as the helicopter settled in above the dirt landing. Thick clouds of ore dust choked the air.

"Get on your feet, Gordo," Red ordered. "And don't be complaining none about being snake bit."

With some help from Pirate, Gordo got to his feet.

The helicopter landed with a gentle bump, and Hathaway immediately opened the cockpit door and climbed out. Ducking his head as the blades slowed, he came over to where his half-brothers were standing near the fire.

"Nice to see you, Hathaway," Red said in as cordial a voice as he could muster.

"Has the mission been completed?" Hathaway said, in no mood for small talk, his gaunt, pointed face the picture of wickedness.

"Partly," Red replied with a silly, nervous grin.

"And what exactly does partly mean?" Hathaway's narrow-set eyes were fixed in a deadly stare at his redheaded half-brother.

"It means we only got two of them kids," Red confessed with a mousy smile.

"I reckon you'd call it a case of bad timing," Gordo said. "That there boy wasn't in the bunkhouse when we sneaked in and snatched up them little gals, and on top of that I went and got myself snake bit." He pulled up the leg of his pants. "Hurts something awful."

Red flashed a despicable sneer at his bloated brother. "You're an idiot," he muttered.

"Thanks for that captivating medical report, Gordo," Hathaway said. "I'm sure we all really care."

"Gordo's right," Red conceded grudgingly, "the boy weren't, you know, there."

"So where was he?" Hathaway asked pointedly.

"We got them little gals sure enough, but the third kid wasn't in the bunkhouse," Red replied. "We searched that bunkhouse from one end to the other, and he wasn't there. Nothing but them two little gals and one big snake."

"You didn't answer my question," Hathaway said, his face flushed with anger.

Red shook his head. He tried to hold his brother's malicious gaze, but couldn't. "Don't know," he said, looking away.

Hathaway was stone cold silent for several long seconds as he allowed the anger to drain from his face. Then he said, "Where's the girls?"

"Pirate done dumped 'em into a mine shaft." Red waved

a finger at the entrance to the mine. "Leastwise, he said he dumped 'em into a mine shaft."

"What do you mean by that?" He looked at Pirate, and then turned back to Red.

Red cast a distrustful glance at Pirate. "It means I ain't so sure."

***

A tiny, almost inaudible *Crunch* broke the stillness of the mine, and in the patchy darkness, Pia whispered, "Did you hear something, Kiki?"

Pia and Kiki were hunkered down inside the ore cart, their backs against the rusty iron sides of the four-wheel wagon. The roar of the helicopter had echoed down the tunnel minutes earlier. It had been a loud, frightening sound, but now it was quiet.

Well, almost quiet.

"No, what did it sound like?" Kiki asked.

Pia listened intensely, but there was only silence. "Nothing. I guess it was nothing."

"Maybe a rat." They had seen a big one earlier scurrying down the tunnel.

"I hope it wasn't a rat," Pia replied in a soft voice.

"It's not the Ragland brothers," Kiki said in a quiet voice. "They think Pirate threw us down that mine shaft."

"You don't think he was tricking us?"

Kiki nodded in the darkness. "No."

Suddenly, the odd sound returned.

Crunch!

It was louder this time.

"Hear it?" Pia said.

"Yes, but I don't know—"

"Kiki…?"

"I know," Kiki said. There was a long pause as Pia and Kiki looked at each other in the spotty darkness. "We're moving."

Chapter 20

"You boys had one simple task," Hathaway was saying, the corners of his mouth curled into a snarl. "Kidnap the three brats, bring them to the mine, and dump them into the shaft." He looked at each of them. "Now is that so hard to do?"

"Bad timing," Gordo repeated. "If that there boy had of been in the bunkhouse, we'd—"

"Well, Gordo," Hathaway snarled, wringing his bony hands, "he wasn't and you didn't. So what do we do now?"

"I reckon we, uh, well…" Gordo had no answer. "Leg's hurting again," he muttered, shifting his weight and favoring his good leg. He heaved a big sigh. "Hurts something awful."

Red flashed an awkward grin at his raw-boned half-brother. "Maybe once that boy learns them little gals ain't around no more, he'll think twice about taking pictures of them glyphs."

Hathaway turned to Pirate, who had been strangely

quiet. "What do you have to say about all this, my one-eyed half-brother?"

"Red's right as rain," Pirate replied in a cheery voice. "It don't make no sense that boy would want to sketch them glyphs and such when he knows how dangerous it'd be."

Hathaway paused, and then said to Red, "Pirate did the dirty deed?"

Pirate said: "I pushed them into the mine shaft. About twenty feet down to the water. No way they're getting out. They was—"

"But I didn't hear no splash," Red said, his eyes fixed on Pirate.

"There was a splash. I guarantee—"

Pirate's fictitious account of the episode was interrupted by an odd crunching noise that originated from the tar-black entrance to the tunnel. All four men turned and peered curiously at the entrance to the mine.

Crunch! Crunch! Crunch!

"What the...?" Red said.

The ghostly noise grew louder. It had the texture of metal grinding metal.

"What's that noise?" Hathaway demanded.

Red leveled a finger at the mine entrance. "Don't know, but it's coming from inside the mine."

A rusty ore cart suddenly emerged from the shadowy mine entrance, its wheels freed for the first time in decades from the rusty bonds that had anchored it to the rails. The iron wheels were spinning faster and faster, and discarding rust with each revolution.

Dumbfounded, the Ragland brothers stared at the ore cart. It was obvious from the perplexed expressions on their faces that they didn't know what to make of an antique ore wagon mysteriously emerging from the tunnel under its own power, and no one made a move to stop it.

Inside the ore cart, Kiki had instructed her cousin to keep her head down. But curiosity had gotten Pablo's sister into more than a few jams in her life, and when the cart was halfway across the landing, Pia raised up and peeked over the side.

Seeing Pia, a chorus of shouts arose from the men (with the exception of Pirate) and Red began running after the ore cart. Gordo limped along on one leg the best he could.

"Don't let them get away!" Hathaway screamed insanely.

Red Ragland raced across the landing and down the tracks in pursuit. Even though he was slowed by his footwear —cowboy boots were not designed for footraces—he quickly closed the distance between himself and the small iron wagon.

"I'll get you!" Red screamed. "And when I do…!"

From inside the wagon, Pia and Kiki had found a supply of ammunition on the rusty floorboard—it was covered with chunks of ore the size of baseballs—and they began hurling the rocks at their pursuer. One grazed Red's head, and another hit his knee.

"When I catch you little brats…!" he screamed, dodging the onslaught of rocks.

"No, you won't!" Pia screamed, launching another projectile in Red's direction.

In the next moment, Red's predicament grew worse. Not only was it raining jagged hunks of mine ore, but now a three-legged dog was matching him stride for stride, barking and nipping at his legs. The animal had appeared from nowhere. Red kicked at the mongrel dog mid-stride, but his canine pursuer fell back, circled, and attacked again from the rear. Red stopped, picked up a rock and threw it at the dog; the animal gave a farewell bark and ran into the forest.

Red resumed the chase, but he had lost valuable time. His spirits lifted, however, when he saw the ore cart beginning to slow.

Finding his second wind and racing to catch up, Red Ragland was within a few feet of the wagon—Pia and Kiki had exhausted their supply of rocks—when the amusement-like-ride reached the steep incline leading away from the dirt landing and down the mountain. In the next moment the getaway vehicle was speeding away and out of Red's reach. He staggered to a halt at the crest of the incline, his face contorted with anger.

"I told you so!" Pia yelled.

"Nice try, Henry Ragland!" Kiki shouted.

Red cursed loudly, and then turned and shouted at Gordo, who hadn't gotten very far. "Saddle the horses!" Gasping for breath, Red then pointed a finger at Pirate, who had remained at the campsite. "I'll deal...I'll deal with you later!"

"I want them caught!" Hathaway yelled, hurrying toward his helicopter. "Failure is not an option!"

Chapter 21

Pablo jumped to his feet, raised a fist, and cheered. "Go Pia! Go Kiki!"

He and Charlie had remained at the edge of the forest a few yards away from the narrow-gauge tracks. They had watched the ore cart and its two passengers emerge from the Jane Sloan Mine tunnel, roll across the landing and down the steep incline. Pablo and Charlie watched in amazement as the ore wagon outpaced Red Ragland's labored dash.

Pablo's first instinct was to rush over to the tracks, grab the ore wagon as it rolled past, and then drag it to a stop.

As he ran toward the tracks, his mind's eye recreated the scene at the end of the rails near the abandoned ore processing plant. There was nothing but air. The narrow-gauge rails and the trestle that had once supported that section of track had collapsed years ago, and once the iron buggy reached that section of rail, it would fly through the air and crash into the side of the building thirty feet away.

Pablo had to prevent that from happening.

He reached the tracks a few seconds ahead of the ore wagon. It was wobbling down the tracks toward him at an alarming speed, and it suddenly occurred to Pablo (and it's a good thing that it did) that if he tried to stop the heavy iron wagon with his bare hands, well, it would probably rip his arms out of their sockets. Or worse, derail the wagon and throw both occupants to the ground. There was simply no way he could bring the heavy wagon to a safe stop. He would have more luck stopping a charging elephant.

Even from a distance—Pia and Kiki were drawing closer and closer each second—Pablo could plainly see sister and cousin. Gripping the sides of the cart, they were standing up, their faces now filled with dread. Their hair was stream-ing in the wind.

Pia held out her hand and shouted to her brother as the cart sped past: "Pablo, help!"

As the ore wagon raced past, Pablo considered scream-ing "Jump!" But he quickly dismissed the idea. The cart was simply going too fast. There was no way Pia and Kiki could jump without hurting themselves. A broken leg or two came to Pablo's mind. Then they would be at the mercy of the Raglands.

As Pablo stood watching the buggy race down the hill, he noticed something sticking up from inside the cart. It was a long wooden handle. Pablo could plainly see that it was attached by metal rods to brake pads near the rear wheels. It was a handbrake!

Pia and Kiki were still within shouting distance, and Pablo yelled, "Kiki, pull the brake!" Pablo raised his arm and pulled an invisible brake.

Kiki responded immediately, grabbing the wooden handle and throwing her shoulder into it. The handbrake did its job, locking onto the rear wheels. The rusty wheels made an awful screeching noise—sparks were flying. The wagon began to slow, but then the wooden handle broke in Kiki's hands and she fell backward onto the floor of the cart and out of sight. The brake pads released, and the ore wagon continued down the mountain, gaining more and more speed.

Then, from behind him, Pablo heard Charlie's voice: "Pablo! To the horses!"

Pablo and Charlie Pecos ran back to their horses. Pablo quickly untied Buster and Charlie removed the hobble from Moses. They swung up into the saddles and urged their horses down the mountain. Over his shoulder, Pablo glimpsed Red as he raced toward his unsaddled horse.

We have a couple minutes' head start, Pablo told himself.

Atop his muscular Paint, Pablo galloped down one side of the rails, and Charlie and Moses raced at full speed down the other. The ore cart continued to fly down the mountain ahead of them.

Terrified, Pia and Kiki stood in the back of the iron wagon watching Pablo and Charlie approach. Barking with every long stride, Sampson the Wonder Dog followed Moses. The three-legged mutt was making amazingly good time.

At a section of terrain where the mountainous incline flattened—it cut through a grassy meadow—the ore wagon slowed, and Pablo and Charlie closed the gap quickly. They were now within twenty yards of the rusty wagon.

Pia and Kiki had figured out the plan, and they were ready to make the leap onto the galloping horses. Her legs dangling over the side, Pia was perched precariously on the left side of the ore wagon—Pablo and Buster's side—and Kiki had taken a place on the opposite side, her legs also dangling, waiting for Charlie and Moses.

The ore wagon left the grassy meadow and began once again to accelerate down a steep section of mountain.

I can't allow the ore cart to reach the end of the tracks, Pablo thought anxiously.

Moses was faster than Buster, and Charlie Pecos had galloped to within ten yards of Kiki. Hunched over his caramel-colored Mustang like some daredevil jockey, Charlie's ponytail flagged in the breeze.

Pablo watched, fearful that it might all go wrong. It would not be an easy maneuver for Pia and Kiki. It would be difficult. Dangerous was a better word. Pia and Kiki would have to stand up on the side of the wagon and jump, all in one quick and seamless motion. It wouldn't be that far for them to jump, but it would require a great amount of coordination. One tiny slip by either of them, and...well, Pablo didn't want to think about it.

Wobbling from side to side like a two-dollar carnival ride, the ore wagon regained the speed it had lost in the grassy meadow, the clattering of the iron wheel growing louder with every revolution.

Charlie pressed forward.

He was within a few short feet of the ore wagon when a tangle of underbrush suddenly loomed ahead of him, and Charlie jerked the reins to the right, losing valuable time as he and the speedy Mustang made the detour. By the time he returned to the tracks, Pablo had taken the lead.

Pablo glanced ahead. No underbrush on his side. No trees. Then he saw the ore plant's tall brick chimney. It rose above the tree line in the distance. Pablo judged it less than a quarter of a mile away—he had plenty of time to rescue Pia.

Nonetheless, he gave Buster another gentle nudge with his boots, and the brown big Paint summoned a new burst of speed. In a few short moments, Pablo was galloping along side the ore buggy.

"Jump, Pia!" Pablo shouted to his sister, who was preparing to stand up. "I'll catch you!" He gripped the reins with one hand, and extended his other hand toward his sister.

"Promise?" Pia cried, her eyes wide and filled with fear, her poncho flapping in the wind.

"Yes, I promise!"

And with that, nine-year-old Pia Perez stood up on the side of the cart, balanced herself for a split second, wobbled slightly, and then leaped. It was a strong, well-timed jump, and Pablo plucked his sister out of the air, gathering her to his chest.

"Sit behind me!" Pablo yelled.

Pia slithered her tiny body around her brother, sat behind him, and then wrapped her arms around his waist.

"Thank you, Pablo!" Pia gasped, her eyes still bugged with fright.

Pablo slowed Buster to a trot, and Charlie and Moses raced past, and in a few seconds they had once again over-taken the ore wagon. The Apache cowboy extended his hand toward Kiki, who was preparing to stand up.

The drab face of the abandoned ore plant loomed into view ahead.

The agile Mustang that Charlie had named Moses was as surefooted an animal in all of New Mexico. Not once in his lifetime of five years had Moses ever lost his footing. He was, after all, a wild mustang. Wild mustangs learned to take care of themselves on the open prairie, and not once had he ever tripped and fallen.

But Moses had never stepped into a groundhog's hole.

Charlie saw the fresh burrow at the last second, but there was no time to react, and Moses' right front hoof dropped squarely into the deep hole. The Mustang lurched forward, ejecting Charlie Pecos.

Moses hit the ground chest-first, careened sideways, and then slid down the steep, grassy incline on his back, his powerful legs pawing at the air, his high-pitched snorts echoing through the forest. Moses quickly climbed to all fours, frightened but unharmed.

Charlie had landed face-first in the grass. The sudden impact had emptied his lungs and a great expanse of air cleared his throat as his world spun out of control. Charlie raised his head for a split second, gasping for air, and then lapsed into unconsciousness.

Pablo had watched in horror as the drama unfolded ahead of him, and as he galloped past the unconscious Apache cowboy, he glanced down at him. Pablo was hoping to see the old man raise his head or move a leg or open his eyes. But Pablo saw none of this.

"Charlie!" Pia cried from the back of Pablo's horse, her eyes riveted on the motionless figure of Charlie Pecos.

When Pablo turned his attention back to Kiki and the ore wagon—he would have to save her as well—his body was chilled to the bone with a nauseating panic. The deserted processing mill was now less than a hundred yards ahead. Pablo could clearly see the end of the tracks—they came to an abrupt end ten yards from the wooden structure. Kiki and the ore wagon were seconds away from soaring off the end of the tracks and crashing into the side of the building. Pablo could see it happening in his mind's eye, and there was nothing he could do to prevent it. He would never reach her in time.

"Pablo!" his sister screamed in his ear, "we've got to help Kiki! Ride faster! Hurry!"

But it was hopeless. Pablo could only watch—the sick panic rising in his throat—and as Kiki and the ore buggy flew off the end of the tracks, a thunderous bolt of lightning streaked across the sky.

"KIKI!" Pablo screamed.

***

The bright flash of light and the booming clap of thunder spooked Red Ragland's horse, and the cow pony came to an abrupt halt, pitching the glyph-stealing, kidnapping cowboy forward and nearly throwing him out of the saddle. The horse next began to buck, again nearly dislodging Red, and he tightened the reins and fought to keep the horse under control.

"It ain't nothing but lightning, ya dumb animal!" Red shouted, slapping the horse on the side of its head. "Ain't ya never seen lightning before?"

In a few seconds the horse settled down.

Gordo reined in alongside his brother, and raised his eyes skyward. "Going to storm for sure."

"Did ya see that kid riding?" Red asked excitedly. "I think I seen him...him and that Injun. They was riding after that there ore cart. Where'd that Injun and that kid come from?"

The Ragland brothers had lost valuable time saddling their mounts, and they had ridden only as far as the grassy meadow, which was roughly halfway to the abandoned ore processing plant. They could not see the drama unfolding two miles down the mountain.

"I didn't see nothing, Red. Nothing at all. And my leg— it hurts something awful, Red! Something awful!"

The sky turned as black as night and more thunder echoed off the granite walls of Burro Mountain. A second bolt of lightning crashed into the forest nearby, startling the two horses. They whinnied and pawed at the earth.

"Ain't got no hankering to go chasing after them kids in a lightning storm," Gordo declared. "Bad timing, for sure. And my leg..." He voice fell to a whimper. "I can't hardly stand the pain."

"Ya already said that!" Red growled. "Now shut up and ride!"

***

When the Jane Sloan Ore Processing Plant had been in full production, extracting from the mountain more than seventy-eight tons of silver over a span of several decades, the pair of narrow-gauge railroad tracks had extended down the mountain, through a second-floor entryway and into the plant. The silver ore was dumped from the ore wagons and into a huge, cone-shaped funnel, which was connected to a rock crushing machine on the first-floor landing.

When an Albuquerque man bought the old place and turned it into a museum in 1967, he had covered the second-story ore wagon entryway with a thin sheet of plywood to keep birds from nesting inside.

It was this thin sheet of plywood that Kiki and the ore buggy struck.

Two factors were in Kiki's favor: The wagon was heavy and it was going fast, and when it collided with the plywood, the cast-iron ore cart poked through the wood like it was nothing more than a sheet of tracing paper.

Kiki had ducked down on the floor of the wagon as it flew through the air and penetrated the plywood panel. When it landed with a terrific jolt inside the abandoned ore plant, Kiki was tossed out of the cart and onto the museum floor. The ore buggy continued down a flight of stairs and crashed into a hand-powered Jackson Drill exhibit near the first-floor entrance.

Kiki rolled along the floor, coming to rest beside a glass-enclosed mineral deposit display—her head was swimming. When she came to her senses, she looked up to see the dreadful silhouette of a man standing over her. He held a pick. It was raised and ready to strike.

A deafening clap of thunder shook the walls of the shadowy museum and Kiki recoiled, her eyes focused on the man with the pick. Feeling a wave of dizziness, her head sank to the floor.

***

Standing over Charlie Pecos, Moses nudged the unconscious Mescalero Apache with his nose. A lump the size of a hen's egg had formed on the side of Charlie's head, and a small cut could be seen on his chin. His breathing was shallow. When Charlie failed to stir, Moses nudged him again, but still Charlie did not move.

Moses made a grumbling sound in his throat, threw back his head and snorted, and for a third time nudged his master, and for a third time Charlie Pecos did not move.

Sampson lay nearby, whining softly.

Chapter 22

It started to rain.

Colossal bolts of lightning tore open the clouds, and raindrops the size of grapes began to spiral earthward. One moment the rain came in large drops and in the next in buckets. Lightning and thunder danced across the heavens, and the forest canopy shook from a mighty wind. Leafs were stripped from branches, branches from trees. The fury of the storm was deafening.

With Pia holding tight around his waist, Pablo rode down to the abandoned ore processing plant, and then around to the back of the dilapidated row of cottages that had once been home to the hard-rock miners. His pace was hurried. Pablo rode along the row of cottages until he found one with its roof still intact. There was only one such cottage, and he quickly reined Buster to a halt and slid to the ground. Pablo helped his sister down, and then tied Buster's reins to a large, rusty flywheel that was leaning against the ramshackle cottage.

"Go inside and wait for me, Pia," Pablo told his sister, wiping rain from his face. Anticipating her reply, he said: "And I don't want to argue about it. There's isn't time."

"But what about Charlie, Pablo?" Pia's bottom lip was quivering. "And Kiki? We need to help them." Rain splattered her face.

"That's what I'm going to do, Pia. I'm going to…to help them."

Pablo had no plan. There were simply too many things going on at once. Charlie was injured. Kiki was probably injured, too, maybe seriously. Pablo had seen the ore buggy smash through the plywood wall. He could only guess how well Kiki had survived the impact and the subsequent crash inside. Her injuries could be serious.

And what about the Raglands? They were probably close. And Hathaway and his helicopter?

There were too many things going on at once.

What would Charlie do? Pablo thought.

Pablo had seen some big rainstorms before—Missouri had its share of gully washers—but he had never seen anything quite like this. It was coming down so hard and so fast that the surrounding forest was no more than musty gray shadows. When lightning struck a groove of Aspens off to his left, Pablo could feel the hairs on the back of his neck stiffen from the electrical charge in the air.

He dug his poncho out of his saddlebag and pulled it down over his body.

Through the heavy timber, Pablo could barely make out Dry Creek. It was flexing its muscles. Indeed, it was already out of its banks, churning with whitecaps and rushing down the mountainside.

"You stay inside the shack and out of the rain," Pablo yelled to his sister, who was on the verge of tears. "I'll get Charlie and Kiki."

"Are you just saying that?"

"No, I mean it."

Pia nodded and hurried into the cottage through the back door, and Pablo set out on foot toward the museum to find Kiki.

***

Kiki gazed up at the dark figure before her. She expected the man to drop his pick on her at any moment when a flash of lightning illuminated the stationary figure a second time. It was only a mannequin, a museum piece. Her heart racing, Kiki breathed a nervous sigh of relief and laughed softly. "That is one spooky mannequin."

Kiki got to her feet. With each blinding flash of lightning she took stock of her surroundings. The second floor of the museum was cluttered with various mineral displays and worthless mining equipment: jack hammers, drill bits, shovels, wrenches, chains of various sizes, and all other manner of tools once used to extract the silver from Burro Mountain. Black and white photographs of miners adorned the walls.

Something called a Litter Basket—a small sign identified it—was leaning against the wall near the stairs that led down to the front door. It reminded Kiki of the litters that rescue patrols used to bring injured snow skiers down the mountain. This Litter Basket was once used to bring injured workers out of the mines.

Moving cautiously, she stepped over to the stairway and gazed down at the four-wheel ore buggy that had given Pia and she the ride of their lives. The ore wagon had careened down the stairs and now lay on its side near the museum's front door.

In the next second, Kiki saw (or thought she saw) someone open the front door of the museum. The person stepped inside, leaving the door open.

Kiki crouched low and watched, her head still swimming dizzily, her ears ringing from the clamor of rain beating the tin roof senseless. She blinked, trying to focus her eyes.

Another thunderous lightning bolt shattered the heavens, splashing light into the museum, and Kiki could see a figure in a poncho. Her eyes came into focus.

It was Pablo.

Chapter 23

"Are you okay, Kiki?" Pablo gasped, kneeling beside his cousin.

Pablo had sprinted up the stairs two at a time after Kiki called out his name.

"My right shoulder is a little sore, and I'm sort of dizzy," Kiki replied with a slight grimace. "But what about Charlie, Pablo? He and Moses took a really hard fall. When I looked back he wasn't moving. He wasn't…He couldn't…I'm really, really worried." Her voice cracking with emotion, she placed her hand over her mouth to choke back the sob.

"I know…he took a very hard fall," Pablo said, his tongue so thick with worry that he could hardly get the words out. Pablo was certain the old man had been badly injured. He might have been…well, Pablo didn't want to think the worst.

"Where's Pia?"

Pablo told Kiki that his sister was safe and dry in one of the cottages nearby.

"We should go back for Charlie," Kiki said in a gruff,

raspy voice, the thunder and lightning tearing at the black storm clouds, the splatters of light casting ghoulish figures on the museum walls.

"I don't think his horse was hurt," Pablo said, talking above the rain that was pummeling the tin roof. "Moses got right up like nothing had happened. It was amazing." Pablo looked at Kiki in the spotty darkness. "This dizziness...Are you dizzy now?" He didn't like the sound of it. Kiki might have a concussion.

Kiki nodded faintly. "Maybe a little."

"We'll rest here for a few minutes, and maybe your dizziness will go away."

"What about the Ragland brothers?"

"I didn't see them." No, he hadn't seen them, but Pablo knew they weren't far. And then, remembering, he said, "What were those screams all about in the mine?"

Kiki told Pablo how Pirate had devised a plan to spare their lives.

"He's a good person at heart," Kiki said thoughtfully.

Their attention was diverted downstairs. Eerie cones of light—not lightning, but manmade light—streaked through the open front door below. The whinny of horses punctuated the fury of the storm.

"Pablo...?" Her eyes fixed on the cones of light, Kiki grabbed his hand and squeezed it.

"The Ragland flashlight patrol," Pablo said, touching the rabbit stick in his back pocket. "Do the Raglands have guns?"

Kiki nodded. "Red keeps a rifle in a leather sheath attached to his saddle. I don't know about Gordo."

That should even the odds, Pablo thought to himself, amused. *A rabbit stick versus a rifle.*

At that moment, Red Ragland and his snake-bit brother Gordo stepped inside the deserted museum. Standing in the open door and silhouetted by each bright burst of lightning, the two men immediately began scanning the museum with their flashlights.

"Okay, children," Red yelled above the crashing sound of rain. "We know you're in here. We seen the hole in the back wall, and lookie here, right here next to the door, is that there ore buggy that you little gals used to escape in. Heck, it's plum empty. So where's the little gals that rode it down the hill? Was that the boy I seen riding so hard?" Red crowed. "It's sort of like a family reunion, ain't it? And if my guess is right, everybody is on the second floor. Am I getting warm?"

On their knees and out of sight behind a Grinding Tools display near the top of the stairs, Pablo and Kiki remained quiet. Peeking around the display case, Pablo could make out the figures of Red and Gordo below. A vague film of light from their flashlights spilled onto their ghoulish faces. Gordo kept shifting his enormous weight from one leg to the other.

"Gordo was bitten by a rattlesnake back at the bunkhouse," Kiki told Pablo, her mouth at his ear. "He's pretty bad off."

"Leg hurts something awful," Gordo moaned from below.

Pablo strained to see if Red had a rifle. He couldn't tell one way or the other.

"Oh, and by the way," Red continued in a loud voice, "we seen that Injun feller—that Apache brave. He was all laid out like he was the best man at his own funeral." Red uttered a haunting laugh, and then spit. "I'm guessing he was plum dead. Didn't move none when we rode by."

"They're bluffing," Pablo whispered. "Charlie's tough."

"Heck," Red continued, "he didn't move one bit. If my brother here could talk without moaning he'd say it was bad timing for that Injun brave. Gordo's in a bit of a bad way at the moment, snake bit and all. It was bad timing for him, too."

"Pablo," Kiki whispered in his ear, "what should we do?"

"Nothing," he replied. "Let them make the first move."

A tremendous clap of thunder exploded, shaking the museum to its core. Pablo and Kiki could feel the wooden floor quiver beneath them.

"So is that there boy with you little gals?" Red shouted from below. "Him and you gals make a great team. We seen all three of ya in the canyon several times and again that day when we was butchering that Bar-7 cow." There was a pause. "You three hook up again?"

Pablo and Kiki remained quiet, peeking around the display case, their eyes fixed on the two loathsome cowboys below.

Let them make the first move, Pablo thought. *That's what Charlie would do.*

"If ya come out and don't make me and my snake-bit brother chase after ya, we can get this thing settled," Red continued, yelling above the storm. "Here's the deal. Ya promise not to take no more pictures of them glyphs, and me and my brother here will promise not to hurt ya none. How's that sound?"

Pablo again peeked around the display case. He could see the two men talking, but he couldn't make out what they were saying. A dagger of lightning crashed into the forest nearby—it was like a thousand electronic flashes on a thousand cameras going off at once—and Pablo could now see that Red had his rifle cradled in his arms.

"What now?" Kiki whispered.

"Patience."

"Another thing," Red shouted, "Pirate didn't throw ya little gals into that there mine shaft 'cause I told him not to. We was just trying to scare ya. That's all. Just scare ya."

"He's lying, Pablo," Kiki said into Pablo's ear.

"I know."

Pablo could make out the Ragland brothers talking in low voices. Choking on his words, Gordo bemoaned the terrible pain in his leg.

"Okay," Red began again, "we tried being nice, now we're gonna be nasty. I don't want to be nasty. I want to be nice, but you kids ain't cooperating." Another short pause. "I'm gonna count to ten, and if ya ain't where we can see ya by the time I get to ten, well, it ain't gonna be pretty. It's gonna be downright ugly."

"Can't hardly stand the pain," Gordo groaned.

"Pablo, I have an idea," Kiki whispered, gesturing at the Litter Basket a few feet behind them.

"One!...Two!...Three!..."

Pablo smiled. "Sled down the stairs?"

"We've got to get out of here, and I'm guessing that front door is our only choice," Kiki said. "They won't know what hit them."

There was another way out—through the hole in the wall made by the ore wagon. But Pablo knew it was a thirty-foot drop.

"Four!...Five!...Six!..."

"We'll give it a try," Pablo said, and he crawled over and gently removed the Litter Basket from the display rack. He laid it flat on the floor beside them.

"Seven!...Eight!...Nine!..."

Pablo edged the Litter Basket toward the top of the

stairs, and then put his mouth to Kiki's ear. "When I say go we go…into the Litter Basket and down the stairs. It's a straight shot out the front door. Once you get outside, bear to the left. Head for that row of cottages."

"Ten! Time's up! And here we come! I hope you're plum scared 'cause if ya ain't, ya sure enough oughta be!"

Following the beams from their flashlights, Red and Gordo began climbing the stairs. Gordo was limping and groaning with each step.

"You'll see Buster," Pablo told Kiki. "Pia's inside. Now get ready."

Pablo pulled his rabbit stick out of his back pocket. A clamorous bolt of lightning flashed—the accompanying thunder was ear-splitting—and Pablo could see the Ragland brothers plainly. They were halfway up the staircase. Pablo stood up, pushed the Litter Basket closer to the stairs, and drew back his arm, his fingers lightly gripping one end of the rabbit stick. He waited for the next flash of lightning.

Not yet. Patience.

Three things happened at once: Lightning lit the muse-um. Gordo saw Pablo and cried out, "There he is, Red! Shoot him!" Pablo released his rabbit stick.

The boomerang-like device flew true and straight, striking Red Ragland in the bridge of his nose. Crying out in pain, Red dropped his flashlight and then his rifle, and his hands immediately flew to the gaping wound in his nose. It was bleeding profusely. He stepped back, lost his balance, and tumbled down the stairs.

"Now!" Pablo yelled, and he and Kiki jumped into the Litter Basket. Pablo sat in front and Kiki dropped in behind him.

The Litter Basket balanced on the top step for a moment, and then tipped forward and flew down the stairs like a plastic sled on a snowy hill. It was another case of bad timing for Gordo. He clearly saw the basket coming at him—he had the two kids centered in the beam from his flashlight—but the behemoth Ragland brother was slow to react, and the sled struck him in his good leg, whipping it out from under him. Gordo uttered a painful shriek and rolled down the stairs, coming to rest on top of his injured brother.

Pablo and Kiki rode the Litter Basket out the open front door and into the New Mexico rainstorm. The cold rain hitting their faces, they jumped to their feet.

"Go!" Pablo said.

Following Pablo's instructions, Kiki ran as fast as her legs would carry her, splashing water with each hurried stride, around the old wooden museum toward the cottages.

The Ragland brothers had tied their horses to a small tree outside the museum. Pablo quickly untied the horses, gave a scream and a yell and threw up his arms, and the horses bolted into the stormy morning grayness.

Pablo raced toward the cottages. He found Kiki at one end of the rotting shacks.

"Where's Buster?" Kiki said, desperation in her voice. "You said he was outside!"

A sheet of lightning bathed the cabins with midday light, and Pablo scanned the rear of the cottages. Buster was gone.

"Pia!" Pablo yelled, feeling sick to his stomach.

The storm continued.

***

Red and Gordo were knotted together at the foot of the museum stairs like two pieces of wet spaghetti. Cursing loudly, Red pulled himself free of the entanglement and got to his feet. He was bleeding from his nose. "When I catch that kid…!" he roared.

"Leg hurts something awful," Gordo moaned, pulling himself up on one elbow.

"I don't want to hear that again!" Red barked. "Now git up!"

"That kid had some sort of…some sort of flying stick," Gordo said, gasping for breath.

"Don't ya think I know that, ya idiot? That flying stick done broke my nose." Red's bloody face was contorted with anger. "Now git up!"

"They rode down the stairs on some sort of sled." Gordo

crawled over to the ore wagon, and used it to pull himself to his feet. "Bad timing I'd say. Knocked my good leg plum out from under me."

"You're an idiot!"

"Never felt so bad in all my life, Red. Almost wish I'd just die," Gordo croaked. "The pain is terrible bad."

***

Pablo hurried to the cottage where he had left Pia. It was easy to find because it was the only cottage with a roof. Kiki was a step behind. When Pablo arrived at the cottage, he opened the back door and looked inside—his spirits lifted. His sister was seated in one corner, Buster's reins in her hands. Pia had brought the muscular brown and white Paint inside with her.

"Pia, you scared me to death," Pablo gasped, rushing in.

Pia spotted Kiki immediately, and she jumped to her feet. "Kiki! You're okay!" Pia dashed over and threw herself into her cousin's outstretched arms. "I was afraid you were…"

"I'm fine, Pia, thanks to Pablo."

"Why'd you bring Buster inside, Pia?" Pablo asked. "I told you to—"

"He was getting all wet, Pablo" Pia said sheepishly, her teeth chattering. "I'm cold and I thought he might be cold, too. Was that okay? That I brought him inside?"

Pablo nodded. "It was okay…" He patted Buster gently on the neck. "Can you carry all three of us, big boy?"

Buster's skin quivered and he tossed back his head and snorted.

"If we go back for Charlie," Pablo began anxiously, looking at Kiki, "the Raglands might—"

"We have to go back for Charlie," Kiki said, a determined tone to her voice. "He tried to save me. I should, we should, go back for him."

"We can't just leave him there, Pablo," Pia insisted. "He's hurt really bad."

Whatever I do, I'd better do it quick, Pablo thought.

"How's the dizziness, Kiki?" Pablo asked, looking into her glassy eyes.

Kiki tried to put on a brave face, but Pablo could see through it. "It's better. Not as bad as before."

A lightning bolt struck in the forest nearby—it was no more than fifty yards away—and it startled them.

"Pablo, that w-was c-close!" Pia stammered. She was shivering under the poncho.

What would Charlie do?

"Okay, all aboard," Pablo said, swinging up into the saddle, and then giving Pia and Kiki a hand. They settled in behind Pablo. Pia's arms were snug around her brother, and Kiki's arms were wrapped tightly around her nine-year-old cousin. Pablo could feel his sister's body twitching from cold. Her teeth were rattling in his ear.

It's really like carrying only two riders, Pablo thought. The combined weight of Pia and Kiki is really only that of one additional rider. Buster's carrying two people, not three, Pablo imagined, trying to put a positive spin on a negative situation. Yeah, two not three.

"You can do it, boy," Pablo said, giving Buster a nudge with his boot.

Buster nudged the back door open with his nose, and everyone ducked their heads as the stallion walked slowed out the rear of the cottage and into the rainstorm. The lightning and thunder continued to tear holes in the black morning sky.

The cold rain dripping off his hat, Pablo reined Buster to a halt at the end of the row of weathered shacks. From that vantage point, looking back up the mountain, Pablo could see the general area where Charlie and Moses had taken their terrible fall.

Although the mountain terrain was stained with shadows —the storm clouds swirled around them like dusty devils gone wild—Pablo could make out the vague outline of Moses. The athletic Mustang stood like a stone monument, fixed and unmoving.

Pablo's attention was diverted. Off to his left, in the heavy timber adjacent to the mountain of chat and not too far from where Moses stood, Red and Gordo had found their horses and were preparing to mount them.

Pablo gave Buster another nudge, and the stallion broke into a trot, past the deserted museum and down the mountain. "Take us home, Buster." Pablo gave the big Paint another nudge with his boot and the brown and white stallion went from a trot to a canter.

"Pablo!" Pia cried, "you're going the wrong way!"

Pablo didn't answer for the longest time. "I know, Pia."

"PABLO! NO!" Kiki cried.

Chapter 24

Pablo slowed Buster to a walk, and the trip down the mountain was agonizingly slow. The stinging rain continued to sweep over them like cold ocean waves. No one spoke. Each of them was thinking about Charlie Pecos and Pablo's decision to leave him on the mountain. Pablo was filled with a deep sense of guilt. It made perfect sense that the safety of his sister and cousin were more important than helping Charlie, but nonetheless Pablo was overcome with regret. He could not shake it from his mind.

Every few minutes Pablo would glance back over his shoulder expecting to see two riders on horseback, but the glyph-stealing Ragland brothers were nowhere to be seen. Pablo had no hope that the brothers would lose Buster's trail. The hoof prints made deep impressions in the wet soil, one even a blind man could follow. Besides, the brothers knew where Buster and his passengers were headed.

It continued to rain, the thunder and lightning ripping the black sky to pieces.

***

Buster moved down the valley, following the flooded outline of Dry Creek, sometimes at a trot, at other times a walk. His three passengers crowded together to stay warm. Pablo and Pia had ponchos, but Kiki was wearing the jacket Pirate had given her the night before—it was soaked. Pia offered to share her poncho, and they both somehow managed to squeeze into it.

They resembled some freak show oddity—one body, two heads.

The farther down the valley they rode, the wider, deeper, and more savage Dry Creek became, and by the time they emerged from the Burro Mountain foothills and rode out onto the prairie, it was a raging torrent more than fifty yards wide. The brown, muddy water churned its way east across the plains, carrying all manner of debris—logs and bushes, mostly—and when they reached the spot where they needed to cross, Dry Creek was a deep, fast-moving river. Wide swatches of riverbank were being sucked into the powerful current.

The hard rain continued.

Kiki said it first. "What now, Pablo?" Her hair fell over her face in stringy tangles, and her lips were the color of plums.

Pablo had no answer.

A lightning bolt struck a nearby piñon tree, slicing it apart.

"Pablo, I can f-f-feel my heart b-b-beating," Pia said, sneaking a glance at the smoldering tree, her teeth continuing to chatter. "That was r-r-really c-c-close."

Kiki's question pestering his thoughts—"*What now, Pablo?*"—Pablo studied the turbulent waters and weighed his options.

"Pablo, look!" Kiki cried. She was gazing over her shoulder and pointing back up the trail.

Pablo turned in his saddle. A rider was emerging from the murky curtain of rain.

"Is it Charlie?" Kiki asked hopefully.

"Can't tell," Pablo replied, wiping the rain from his eyes.

"It's Charlie, Pablo!" Pia cheered.

The lone rider spurred his mount. Pablo watched as the man removed a rifle from its scabbard.

"No, it's not, Pablo!" Kiki cried. "It's Red Ragland! He's going for his rifle!"

***

Gordo had made a mess of things. After Red and his over-weight brother caught their horses near the chat pile adjacent to the deserted Jane Sloan processing mill, they had mounted up, and then headed down the mountain in pursuit of the three kids who had brought their glyph-stealing activities to a grinding halt.

They hadn't ridden very far—no more than few hundred yards—when Gordo fell from his horse. Under normal circumstances, Red would have gone on without his brother, but Gordo had caught his foot in the stirrup, and he was being dragged down the mountain. Even Red Ragland could not bear to see such a sight, and he had chased down Gordo's mount, reined it in, and then dismounted and freed his younger brother from the stirrup.

Although Gordo had cost Red valuable time, Red's prey was now in sight, and he held firm to his rifle and spurred his mount forward.

***

Earlier, inside his Bell 407 helicopter, Truman Hathaway, alias Harvey Ragland, had just lifted off and was headed down the mountain in search of the three young trouble-makers when a thunderbolt struck his aircraft, racing through the electrical system at the speed of light.

The dishonest Santa Fe businessman believed luck to be on his side because the helicopter did not appear to be damaged. A few seconds later, however, as the thunder and lightning exploded all around the helicopter, the emergency dashboard light flashed on. The four-blade rotary system had malfunctioned, and the aircraft was losing power. The cabin was filling with smoke and the smell of burnt rubber.

Hathaway was a good pilot, and although his instruments were erratic—the emergency buzzer was ringing insanely—he was confident he could squeeze enough power out of the Bell 407 to make the return trip to the Santa Fe Municipal Airport. It was only a twenty-minute flight. He would deal with the three mischief-makers later.

When the helicopter began to lose altitude, however, Hathaway broadcast a Mayday alert on his aircraft radio and prepared himself for the worst. He was losing altitude. Ten seconds later, with the thunder and lightning crashing around him, his helicopter struck the ground. Hard.

Hathaway was lucky to have survived the terrible accident because his helicopter resembled a giant pretzel. How he managed to free himself from the wreckage was nothing short of a miracle. But he had.

The blood from a deep gash in his forehead poured into both eyes and made it almost impossible for him to see. Half-dead and delirious, Hathaway stumbled across the prairie, a torrent of rain dogging his every step. Lightning cracked above his head, and the clamor of thunder crashed in his ears. Swiping at the blood and rain in his eyes, he was overcome by a sick dizziness.

Images were difficult to make out in the monsoon-like storm, and after a few short minutes into his journey, Hathaway came upon what he believed to be a herd of Pronghorn antelope. Clearing the cobwebs from his brain, he peered into the stormy darkness. Yes, it was a herd of antelope. They had been lying down—waiting out the storm—but now they climbed to their feet and advanced towards him. A cold fear gripping his heart, Hathaway began to run, staggering across the prairie mud like some drunken fool.

"Go away!" he cried, looking back over his shoulder as the herd approached at a full gallop. Clods of mud flew into the air from their hoofs.

Harvey Ragland continued to run until he suddenly felt himself adrift, as if he were flying. No, not flying—falling.

Then everything went black.

It continued to rain.

***

"Hang on!" Pablo cried, giving Buster a healthy boot in his side.

"I hope you're not doing what I think you're doing," Kiki said in a loud voice, her arms wrapped firmly around Pia, who was clinging to her brother like some hungry carnivore.

"We've run out of options!" Pablo yelled as a large section of the riverbank broke off and fell into the raging floodwaters just a few feet away.

Buster was a strong, obedient horse, but the sight before

him was frightful, and he responded to Pablo's kick with a combative snort. But Pablo was persistent, and he kept the reins tight and gave the brown and white Paint a second kick in the ribs.

"Come on, Buster!" Pablo urged. "Don't fail me now!"

Red Ragland was now within fifty yards.

The six-year-old Paint named Buster paused at the edge of the floodwaters, flared his nostrils and snorted again, and then rocked back on his hind legs and made a mighty leap into the floodwaters. Pia uttered a shriek as Buster hit the water, squeezing her brother so tight that Pablo struggled to draw a full breath.

"I have a bad feeling about this, Pablo!" Kiki yelled, holding tight to Pia and balancing herself against the cold swirl of water that was pulling at all of them.

"Pablo...!" Pia howled, tightening her grip on him.

Buster did his best to swim forward and fought to keep his head above the muddy water. But the current was merciless, and he and his three passengers were being carried downstream at an alarming pace.

Pablo turned in the saddle and looked back at Red Ragland. The Axe Handle outlaw had dismounted at the edge of the floodwaters. He had dropped to one knee, pushed his hat back on his head, and was now cocking his lever-action rifle.

Beneath the water, Pablo dug his boots into Buster's ribs and gave a mighty kick. "Come on, Buster! You can do it!"

Buster battled the force of the flood as best he could, but his head and nostrils were no more than a few inches above the water. He was sinking fast.

"Go, Buster!" Pia screamed.

When Buster's head sank below the frothy water, Pablo pulled back on the reins, raising the stallion's head. For a few moments, the powerful cattle-horse beat back the current—his legs dug frantically through the cold, muddy water.

"Atta boy!" Pablo encouraged.

"Go, Buster!" It was Kiki.

Pablo expected to hear the burst of a rifle at any moment, and he wasn't disappointed.

The crack of Red Ragland's rifle shot was followed a split second later by the hiss of the bullet scorching the air inches above their heads.

"Down!" Pablo yelled, and his sister and cousin flattened out as best they could against Buster's backbone.

Pablo turned in the saddle and snatched another glimpse of Red Ragland. He had cocked his lever-action rifle a second time and was raising it to his shoulder when the section of riverbank on which he knelt suddenly gave way and fell into the river, dumping him into the swirling water. Ragland uttered a muffled scream as the angry floodwaters sucked him under.

In the next moment, a splotch of red hair could be seen bobbing up and down in the swift water. Red Ragland was digging at the water with his arms. The last thing Pablo saw was the New Mexico cowboy clawing at the muddy riverbank.

Their good fortune was brief, however, because the strength of the floodwaters and the weight of three riders were too much for the Bar-7 Paint. When Buster's head dipped below the water a second time, Pablo slithered out of the saddle and into the water. Buster's head immediately rose and he and his passengers shot forward, the stallion's legs renewed by the discharge of weight.

"Pablo!" Pia screamed, her face wrenched with fear. "Don't leave us!"

"Pia, you and Kiki move up!" Pablo screamed, dog-paddling alongside Buster as best he could. "Grab the saddle horn!" Swimming in a poncho was impossible, and he pulled it over his head and allowed the water to take it.

Pia was clearly confused, and she hesitated for a moment before moving forward and into the saddle. She and Kiki were still sharing the same poncho, and Pia's cousin scooted in behind her. Pia immediately fished around in the cold water for the reins.

"Grab hold, Pablo!" Kiki shouted, extending her hand.

"No! Buster can't..." Buster can't swim with three riders, is what Pablo wanted to say, but the water was spinning, trying to pull him down, and talking was the last thing on his mind at the moment. Keeping his head above water was the first.

Pablo swallowed a mouthful of water and gagged momentarily. The water tasted bad and broke the rhythm of his swim. He tried to keep pace with Buster, but in a few short seconds, the powerful stallion and his sister and cousin were well ahead. They were now more than halfway across the swollen creek.

Pablo fought the powerful current. His lungs were on fire and the muscles in his arms and legs burned with pain. Pushing through the panic that gripped him, Pablo kicked and pulled at the water savagely. But it was a losing battle. The water was winning.

A white-hot bolt of lightning split the sky directly above Dry Creek. The electrical charge warmed the air, and the shockwave caused Pablo's ears to pop.

When a rotting piñon tree floated past, Pablo grabbed onto it. He laid his head against the piñon and fought to catch his breath. His teeth were chattering and his muscles were in the grip of one continuous tremor. He was bone weary and each small movement required superhuman strength.

Something caught Pablo's eye at the other end of the piñon tree. It was a slithering ball of gray ribbons. A pang of fear pierced his heart. It was a family of rattlesnakes. Pablo counted five heads.

No, six!

But Pablo wasn't frightened. The snakes' tails weren't rattling and their tongues weren't flicking. They were too wet and cold to put up a fight. They were simply trying to survive.

"You guys stay on your end of the tree," Pablo muttered, "and I'll stay on mine."

The storm continued to release its fury—it had been pent up for one hundred and twenty-two days—and visibility was cut to no more than a few hundred feet. Looking back over his shoulder, Pablo spotted the muscular stallion pulling himself out of the water on the opposite riverbank. Pia and Kiki were still aboard. They had made the crossing.

"Good boy, Buster," Pablo whispered.

The cold, turbulent water had sapped Pablo of his energy, and his arms and legs continued to blaze with fatigue. He glanced at the shuddering sphere of rattlers. They were still wrapped around one another trying to stay warm.

Pablo dropped his head against the trunk of the piñon tree and allowed the flood to take him.

***

The rotting piñon tree delivered Pablo to a shallow stretch of water half an hour later. He suddenly felt Mother Earth at his feet, and he pushed away from the log and its family of Diamondback rattlers, and sloshed out of Dry Creek. He had taken only a few steps before he collapsed to the muddy ground from exhaustion. He lay flat on his back in the mud, his chest rising and falling in spasms of heavy breathing. High-pitched gasps trickled up from his throat, and his ears were ringing from fatigue. He was wet and cold.

But I'm alive.

Pablo lay in the mud for the longest time, the rain splattering his face.

When at last the rain quit fifteen minutes later—it had rained for more than four straight hours—Pablo pulled himself to his feet. The place looked vaguely familiar, and when he saw the biggest cottonwood tree in Sierra Vista County he was filled with a rush of energy.

"*Arbol Grande*," he said softly.

In the soft, wet sand, not far from the tree, Pablo saw Buster's fresh hoof prints. The tracks led east toward the ranch.

As Pablo began the ten-mile walk back to the ranch, the clouds pulled apart and the afternoon sun peeked through. A brilliant shaft of light connected sky to Mother Earth like a glistening highway.

The warm sun felt good against his body.

Chapter 25

Charlie Pecos opened his eyes and looked around the room. Pablo and Pia were standing on one side of his bed with their mother. Kiki and her parents stood beside them. Uncle Antonio, Aunt Helen, and Sheriff Maggie Frost were standing on the other side of the bed.

"Where am I?" Charlie asked in a soft, throaty voice. "Is this heaven?"

Uncle Antonio laughed. "No, Charlie, it's not heaven, unless, of course, you believe four inches of rain at the Bar-7 is heaven. It's sure enough heaven for our cows," Uncle Antonio said. "You're at the ranch house."

"The rain...I don't remember the rain," Charlie said, trying to sort through it all. His eyes found Kiki. "I remember riding after young Kiki. She and Pia were in an ore wagon. Moses and Sampson and I were flying down the mountain, and then...I don't remember anything after that."

At the mention of his name, three-legged Sampson the

Wonder Dog jumped onto the bed with Charlie, licking his face, his tail wagging joyfully.

"Hello, old friend," Charlie grinned, wrapping the mutt in his arms.

Sheriff Frost's phone rang, and she excused herself and stepped out of the room.

"Moses tripped, Charlie," Pablo explained. "You and Moses took a terrible fall."

"But Moses jumped right back up!" Pia sang. "He wasn't hurt one bit."

Uncle Antonio said, "You must have somehow managed to climb aboard Moses after you regained consciousness. We were about to send out a rescue party when Moses delivered you to our front door late last night."

"We couldn't..." Kiki stammered. "We didn't..."

"We had to leave you, Charlie," Pablo said, his eyes showing the intense guilt he felt. "The Ragland brothers were mounting up and..." Pablo was unable to complete the thought.

Charlie Pecos raised his hand. "You do not need to explain, Pablo Perez." Smiling, he said, "There is an old Indian saying: 'Better that one should suffer than all should perish.'" Charlie looked at Pablo, his kind, dark eyes sparkling with acceptance. "You did the right thing, Pablo. You showed wisdom."

Pablo shuffled his feet and looked down at the floor. He still felt guilty.

Kiki introduced Charlie to Pablo's mother, and then to her parents.

"We can't thank you enough for all that you've done for the children, Mr. Pecos," Kiki's father said.

"We'll be forever in your debt," her mother said.

"And if you ever get back to Missouri," Pablo and Pia's mother said, "I'll cook you some of my fabulous fajitas."

Charlie seemed embarrassed by all the attention.

Sheriff Frost stepped back into the room. She had some news.

"We'll get no more grief from the Ragland boys," Sheriff Frost said. "My deputy picked up Red Ragland late this morning walking back toward Axe Handle. Pirate came into my office a half-hour ago. Turned himself in." She looked at Kiki. "From what Kiki tells me, Pirate won't do much jail time. Maybe none."

"He saved our lives," Pia said in a small voice.

"Here's another piece of interesting news," Maggie said. "Harvey Ragland crashed his helicopter no more than a quarter mile from Petroglyph Canyon. He managed to crawl out of the wreck, got lost in the storm and fell into the canyon. From the muddy footprints it appeared like he was running."

"Was he…?" Uncle Antonio said.

Maggie Frost nodded.

"He was running from his own demons," Charlie noted.

"My deputy found him. Called in an air ambulance from Santa Fe. Too late to save him." Maggie grimaced. "Gordo wasn't so lucky either. Pirate told my deputy that he died on the mountain. Rattlesnake bite."

"Where is Moses?" Charlie asked, raising up on his elbows and looking concerned.

"Got him hobbled out by the corral," Uncle Antonio said. "I put your saddle and the rest of your gear in the barn."

Charlie threw his legs to the side of the bed and sat up. Uncle Antonio had dressed the Apache cowboy in pajamas.

"Help me to my feet, Pablo."

"Charlie Pecos!" Aunt Helen warned, "You'd better not be moving around too much. That's some knot you've got on the side of your head. You really need to see a doctor."

"Yes, maybe later," Charlie said, extending his hand toward Pablo.

Pablo helped Charlie to his feet.

"Let's go visit Moses," Charlie said. He took a step, wobbled, and paused to regain his balance.

"At least put on some house shoes," Aunt Helen insisted. She set some at Charlie's feet and he slipped into them.

Pablo and Charlie went outside. Charlie's steps were unsteady, but with Pablo's help he managed to navigate around the barnyard puddles to where the Mustang was hobbled near the corral. Pia and Kiki followed. The adults watched from the porch.

"Hello, old friend," Charlie said, walking up to Moses and running his hand the length of the Mustang's nose.

Moses snorted and jostled his head.

"You have proven yourself a loyal companion," Charlie said.

"Back on the mountain he could have run away," Pia observed.

"But he didn't," Kiki added.

"Yes, I know." Charlie stooped down and untied the rope that hobbled the horse's feet.

"Now go, old friend," Charlie said, stepping back and waving his arms over his head. "Go!"

Moses stomped the ground with his front hoofs and uttered a high-pitched whinny. He jostled his head again.

"It is time for you to go back to your wild herd." Charlie waved his arms again. "Go!"

Moses reared, pawed the air with his front hooves, and then turned and galloped across the barnyard toward the open prairie, sprinting like the wind.

They stood watching Moses as he vanished into the distant prairie haze.

"What will you ride now, Charlie?" Pia asked, looking up at the Apache man.

Charlie smiled at Pia. "Charlie Pecos will ride a bus

back to his family on the reservation. His cowboy days are at an end."

"Oh."

Pablo thought he saw tears in Charlie's eyes.

Chapter 26

The 747 passenger jet climbed above the Manzano Mountains east of Albuquerque and headed toward Kansas City. Pablo, Pia, and Kiki sat in the last row of seats. Their parents were seated across the aisle. Kiki was making notes on her phone. Pia seemed deep in thought.

Pablo glanced out the window at the high-plains prairie below. It was green for as far as the eye could see. It was amazing to Pablo how the landscape had changed. One hundred and twenty-two days of drought had made it useless, but one good day of rain had miraculously transformed it into lush, productive pastureland again.

"Pablo," Pia said, her eyes pinched together in concentration, "do you think we'll ever see Charlie Pecos again?"

Pablo turned and looked at his sister. "I'd bet on it, Pia."

Pablo wonder how the prairie might have looked seven thousands years ago, back in a time when Native Americans lived and prospered in Petroglyph Canyon, back in a time when they told their stories on the rocks and walls of that wilderness gorge.

Pia paused to collect her thoughts. "Are you just saying that or do you really mean it?"

Pablo smiled. It had only been a few days, but he already missed the old man. "I really mean it."

The End

About the Author

Award-winning author Christopher Cloud began writing fiction full time at the age of 66 after a long career in journalism and public relations. He graduated from the University of Missouri in 1967 with a degree in journalism, and worked as a reporter, editor, and columnist at newspapers in Texas, California, and Missouri. He was employed by a major oil company as a public relations executive, and later operated his own public relations agency. His 2012 *A Boy Called Duct Tape* was his debut middle-grade novel, and won several literary awards. Chris has also published two young-adult novels: *Voices of the Locusts* in 2013 and *Adelita's Secret* in 2014. Chris lives in Joplin, Missouri. His e-mail address is Chris@ChristopherCloud.com.

Made in the USA
San Bernardino, CA
09 January 2015